"He's just a child," said the formerly rosy-cheeked woman. She was no longer screaming, but her cheeks remained ashen.

"Evil comes in all sizes," said Günter. "You all know that as well as I."

"I-I'm only an orphan," sputtered Bolt. "Or at least I was. But I'll soon be going on picnics and playing water polo with Baron Chordata. Families play water polo together, right?"

No one answered his question, for upon hearing the Baron's name, two more people screamed and one fainted.

"Don't say his name," hissed the bartender.

"He will eat you for dinner. Or maybe lunch!" warned a short man at a table near Bolt. "Or breakfast. I always find a big breakfast is important."

The crowd murmured in agreement.

"Stop scaring the child," said the bartender. "No one knows if the Baron eats children. Not live ones, anyway."

I'm not scared, I'm fierce, Bolt said to himself with as much fierceness as he could muster, which was very little. Surely the Baron could not be as bad as everyone seemed to think.

THE CURSE OF THE
WEREPENGUIN

~→ **Allan Woodrow** ←~

illustrated by Scott Brown

PUFFIN BOOKS

PUFFIN BOOKS
An imprint of Penguin Random House LLC, New York

First published in the United States of America by Viking,
an imprint of Penguin Random House LLC, 2019
Published by Puffin Books, an imprint of Penguin Random House LLC, 2020

Visit us online at penguinrandomhouse.com

Library of Congress Cataloging-in-Publication Data is available
ISBN 9780451480460

Printed in the United States of America

Set in Bell MT Std   Book design by Kate Renner

3   5   7   9   10   8   6   4   2

To M & Em

I know you both don't normally read books like this—scary books, monster books—but I'm dedicating this book to you anyway, and someday, when you have children, many years from now, you can take this off the bookshelf in your house and say, "Look at what your grandfather dedicated to me!" And your children will respond, "Did he write this when he still had hair and teeth?" And you'll answer, "He still had teeth." —A.W.

For my three girls,

Melissa, Ellen, and Emily, and the amazing Maria Fernanda. —S.B.

⌒→ CONTENTS ←⌒

PART TWO
The Transformation

PART THREE
The Curse

PART FOUR
The Attack of the Werepenguin

Prologue: The St. Aves Zoo

Fourteen penguins glared at me with haunting yellow eyes. They seemed disturbed, disdainful, disgruntled, discombobulated, and disagreeably disquieting.

They squawked—loud, roaring barks—beaks frowning.

A chill rose up my back.

I sneezed.

It had been foolish to visit the famed penguin exhibit at the St. Aves Zoo without my handkerchief. My allergy to penguins was even worse than my allergies to zebras, giraffes, monkeys, elephants, emus, tigers, bears, otters, snakes, sheep, cows, various reptiles, and pandas.

Perhaps being a zoo animal procurer had not been the best career choice.

Then again, if I hadn't come to that zoo, on that particular day and at that particular time, I would never have heard the story of the werepenguin. And then, neither would you.

It was late and the zoo was closing soon. I leaned against the railing of the penguin enclosure, twirling the small glass penguin figurine I kept as a good-luck charm. I also carried three rabbits' feet, ten four-leaf clovers, and a framed number seven. Not that I was superstitious, but it never hurts to be prepared.

I sneezed again and needed somewhere to wipe my nose. My sock? My shoelaces? Unfortunately, I was not very flexible.

"Care for this, sir?" asked a man with a large handful of tissues. I yanked one from his grasp.

"Thank you," I said, and then sneezed anew, a tremendous sneeze that sounded like a truck's honk. The man jumped. He seemed nervous, and perhaps bothered by loud noises. I was glad I had left my tuba at home.

"I am the caretaker of the penguins." The fellow was short and round, with an oversize nose and a balding head. He wore a long black overcoat, a black scarf around his neck, and a white shirt. If I squinted, he almost looked like one of the penguins beyond the railing. He slouched, as if he carried a lifetime of worries on his shoulders, and those worries were heavy. Or perhaps he just had weak shoulders.

"I'm here on business," I explained. "Zoo business." The man arched his eyebrows. "I represent a new zoo. A large zoo. A zoo of immense proportions. I have been traveling far and wide, near and thin to purchase animals for the zoo. Your penguins are magnificent. I will buy half of them."

The short, round man frowned. "A kind offer, but I'm afraid you've wasted your travels. The St. Aves penguins are not for sale. They are comfortable here. This is their home."

"Nonsense," I said, and snorted. It was a purposeful snort. "Everything is for sale. May I buy your shoes?"

The man looked down at his black loafers—they looked to be ten sizes too large for him—and shook his head. "No, I'm wearing these. But even if the penguins were for sale, and they are not, I could never sell half of them. They are a family, you see. Families should never be split up."

I scoffed, and then snorted again. "Home? Family? They are birds, sir. They do not need an exhibit as big or as comfortable as this one. You pamper them. All a penguin needs is a cage and some newspapers on the floor."

"Penguins can't read."

"Even so, tell me your price. I must buy your penguins."

I noticed the penguin caretaker was staring at the

penguin figurine in my hand. I held it up for him to see more clearly. "Where did you get that?" he asked.

"At a flea market in Katmandu. They had run out of fleas, so I bought this instead. The man who sold it to me said it was handmade in Brugaria."

"Yes, that penguin is Brugarian. I've seen others like it." The penguin caretaker turned away and looked over the railing. He sighed loudly. "You've heard about the werepenguins of Brugaria, of course."

"Werepenguins? You mean werewolves. Humans who turn into wolves during a full moon."

"Werewolves get all the attention. You don't read as much about the were-aardvarks of Tanzania, or the were-termites of Brazil. Some people call them myths. Who knows? But the werepenguin—now, that's a story."

"Fairy tales," I said with a dismissive wave of my hand. "There's no such thing as were-anything except under-wear. And that's spelled differently."

"May I tell you a story? You may find it even more valuable than our penguins. But I warn you, the tale is long."

"Everyone knows penguin tails are short," I replied, and then chuckled at my joke.

"This is not a story to be taken lightly," he warned. "In fact, I will make you a deal. Listen to my tale. If, at the end, you are still interested in half my penguins, they are yours. For free."

"Free?" I looked at him carefully, to see if he was mocking me. Who ever heard of free penguins? But one look at the man's sunken eyes and saggy cheeks convinced me that he was not someone who told jokes. If he ever had a sense of humor, it had likely been buried long ago. "You have a deal, my friend. Tell me your tale—short or no."

"I warn you, it's a disturbing story. Also, disquieting and discombobulating, like the penguins watching." He gestured to the exhibit, where the waddle of penguins continued to glare at us.

I sneezed, and the man gave me the rest of his stack of tissues. "The story," he said, "starts in a home for abandoned boys. Bolt Wattle was twelve years old, with no family and no prospects for anything except a disappointing future. But his life was about to be changed forever."

"I hate children's stories," I snapped.

"There is nothing childish about this story, I assure you."

PART ONE

The Journey to Brugaria

1.
Purple Pens

The sun had already set while Bolt Wattle waited outside the door of the headmistress's office, afraid to enter. Boys were not often summoned to the office of Headmistress Fiona Blackensmear, and never in the evening.

The headmistress sat in deep concentration at her desk, her forehead knotted, as she examined the sheets of paper atop the open manila folder. Her lips were pursed. Her hair was pinned tight into a bun. Her fingers tapped her desk: pinkie to thumb, pinkie to thumb.

"Have a seat, Humboldt," she said without looking up, her voice as firm as her hair. Her fingers ceased tapping.

Bolt cringed at the sound of his real name. His parents, the parents he had never known, had only left him two things: the name Humboldt, and a stuffed penguin he simply called "Penguin."

He liked the stuffed animal.

Bolt rustled across the floor in his orphanage shoes, two sizes too small and made of burlap, and sat in the green and cracked plastic chair across from the headmistress's desk. He fidgeted. Like his shoes, Bolt's pants were too tight, so he often fidgeted when he sat. The Oak Wilt Home for Unwanted Boys didn't have many clothes for twelve-year-olds.

Nothing else in the room moved. The spiders and moles that roamed the Oak Wilt Home for Unwanted Boys knew better than to enter the office of Headmistress Fiona Blackensmear.

On the desk sat pens nestled inside three clear penholders. The pens were grouped by color: red, black, and blue. Bolt lifted a blue pen and tried to be interested in it but failed. He put the pen back into a penholder.

"Does that belong there?" Ms. Blackensmear growled, her eyes darting up and glaring at the blue pen standing amid the red ones. Bolt was small for his age, and under the headmistress's glare he felt much, much smaller. He moved the pen into its proper holder.

"Better." Ms. Blackensmear slammed her folder shut. "Pens are much like boys, you know. A blue pen is happiest with blue pens like itself. But when that pen is placed incorrectly, such as with red pens, it is distraught." She cleared her throat. "But you are not a blue or a red pen, Humboldt. You are a broken purple pen almost out of ink, one that has only a few more lines left to write before being discarded forever." She tapped each of her fingers again, stared at the folder on her desk, and then back up at Bolt. "But that has now changed."

Bolt blinked, confused. "It has?"

The headmistress stood up, holding the manila folder and waving it with forceful enthusiasm. "Yes! We had a visitor today." Her voice rose in excitement. "A messenger. And he brought this!" She smacked the folder on her desk as if spiking a football after scoring a touchdown. "Do you know what this is?"

"A folder?"

"It is opportunity. We have a request for you. Yes, you specifically. This gentleman doesn't even want to meet you, which is probably for the best." Her eyes wandered to Bolt's neck, where a large bird-shaped birthmark poked out of his shirt collar. Bolt tilted his head slightly to the left, to obscure the mark, as was his habit.

The headmistress looked away, coughed, and then picked up the manila folder once more. "He was quite intrigued by how you ended up with us."

"But I don't know how I got here. I was left at the doorstep as a baby."

"That's what he found so intriguing. It was almost as if you were meant to be together. Isn't that wonderful?"

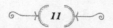

Bolt shivered. He did not think that was wonderful. In fact, he thought quite the opposite. Bolt had always been thankful he was unwanted by prospective parents. He was certain that his family, his real family, was out there somewhere, and would soon return for their long-lost son.

If Bolt left the orphanage, they might never find him.

"But now you can count your chickens," said the headmistress. "They have hatched. For you are to live with a Baron!" If she noticed Bolt's frown, she didn't acknowledge it. "His name is Baron Chordata." After Ms. Blackensmear said his name, Bolt thought he heard a scream, or perhaps a loud squeak from one of the orphanage vermin. He then heard a muffled thud as if the animal, after screaming, had fainted or dropped dead. The headmistress looked down and tapped the folder on her desk. "Yes, a Baron. I don't believe there is a Baroness. A shame, but still, he is practically royalty." She looked back up and smiled. "Your luck runneth over, much like our toilets. I need to get those fixed." She pointed to the door. "You must leave immediately."

"But why would a Baron want me?"

"Maybe you have some royal blood in you." She peered closely at Bolt. "No, that's highly unlikely. Never mind. Perhaps the Baron needs someone to do lab experiments on. Or a houseboy to do his chores. Who knows? Who cares? It's strange and mysterious, but so are many things. Grab your belongings and then you are off to Brugaria."

"Brugaria? Where's that?"

"Far away from here." She jabbed her finger toward the door. "Now, shoo. Assistant Headmaster Smoof is waiting to escort you and ensure you arrive in one piece. Or, at least, that all your pieces arrive at once."

Bolt took a few steps toward the door, his stomach flipping and flopping like a hooked fish. He glanced back at Ms. Blackensmear, who was rubbing a string of pearls she held in her hand. Bolt was quite sure he had never seen her with pearls before.

"It's almost too good to be true," said Ms. Blackensmear, talking to herself. "Of course, if something seems too good to be true, then it probably isn't good at all."

And with that, Bolt walked out the office door, never to return.

2.
A Propensity to Bolt

Bolt peered out the train window and into the inky blackness of the night as the train squealed along rusted tracks. The moon's faint glow revealed a thick but dead forest outside. Tree branches reached out like distorted arms and hands. Ice hung from their fingertips and bits of snow dotted their forearms. They scraped against the train car window as if trying to grab Bolt or poke him in the eye.

Strong winds howled. Somewhere, an animal barked.

Bolt squeezed his stuffed penguin, the one left by the parents he never knew. It had only one wing, with a slight rip and a long char mark where the other wing should have been, as if it had been burned and yanked off. Such had it always been.

Bolt knew he was far too old to be hugging a stuffed animal, but it brought him a small amount of comfort—a very small amount, like using a string for a blanket. Still, it was better than no comfort at all.

They had been traveling for a night and a day; Bolt had hugged Penguin for most of the trip. First, he and Mr. Smoof had caught a plane to New York. Then they'd hopped on a second plane to London, another back to New York when they discovered they were on the wrong plane, and then after two more plane rides, they'd finally climbed aboard this train to Volgelplatz, a fishing village in Brugaria.

Bolt hated every second of the voyage. If people were meant to fly, he felt, they would have been born with wings. The rickety train was just as bad as the planes. It rattled and creaked as if threatening to break in half.

Bolt squeezed his stuffed bird tighter.

Worse, with every click and clack of the rails, and with every takeoff or landing of the planes, Bolt was carried farther and farther away from Oak Wilt. His parents were probably looking for him at that very moment: they had probably arrived at the orphanage mere minutes after Bolt had left.

Across from Bolt slept Mr. Smoof. When awake, the man had been a grumpy companion. Apparently, he was missing his favorite television show, which had something to do with wild animal hunting. Bolt couldn't imagine

Mr. Smoof hunting—he was far too large to sneak around unnoticed, and he smelled like sausages. Surely animals would see him, or sniff him, from miles away.

The man's enormous stomach, and the bright red Christmas reindeer sweater that covered it (it was April, but Mr. Smoof only had so many sweaters), rose up and down as he snored, a grumbling rumble that would have kept the entire train car awake if there had been anyone else in it. But he and Bolt were the train car's only passengers.

Another bark rang out from the darkness outside, savage and primal. Bolt could feel the bark in his bones, like one feels a fog hovering over a frog-infested swamp.

Something about the barks outside the train felt familiar. That was odd, since animals were strictly prohibited at the Oak Wilt Home for Unwanted Boys, with the exception of the spiders, the cockroaches, and the moles. And those creatures were not permitted, just tolerated—and none barked.

Still, it was as if Bolt had heard those barks before. But where? In his dreams?

In his nightmares?

The train hit a nasty bump and its walls shook. Bolt flew a good six inches in the air. This time, surely, the train would break apart, if not from disrepair, then out of spite. Bolt flopped back down on the bench. *TWANG!* A spring broke. The rest of the train held together.

Mr. Smoof continued to snore.

Bolt took a deep breath and told himself that he was fierce. Strong! Like his nickname, he was a thunderbolt crackling with bravery and power.

Bolt hoped that if he told himself those things enough, they might become true. He didn't like to think about the real reason for his nickname, which one of the other orphan boys had given him because Bolt always bolted under his bed when faced with unpleasant things like scary movies or prospective parents coming to adopt someone.

Some of the boys had laughed at Bolt's bolting habit, but he felt it was far better to run away than to stay and face possibly unfortunate consequences.

Just as it would be far better to run, now, back to the orphanage, and into the arms of his parents who might be waiting for him at that very moment. His parents wouldn't care about his strange birthmark or his nose—a nose that Bolt always felt was a little too big—or his unruly hair that seemed to stick up in strange places for no good reason. They would just want Bolt for who he was.

Unless.

Bolt retraced his conversation with the headmistress. *"It was almost as if you were meant to be together." "Maybe you have some royal blood in you."*

As she'd said, it was all so strange. So mysterious.

Unless.

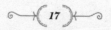

Unless this Baron, this unknown *royalty*, hadn't plucked Bolt at random.

For why else would he have chosen Bolt, sight unseen, unless Bolt had royal blood? Unless this Baron was . . . Bolt's father?

It was all so obvious now.

Bolt sat up straighter. Hope surged in his chest. It was a strange feeling. He had not felt the feeling of hope often, and at first he thought it was a bug that had crawled into his throat, before he realized the feeling was warm and welcoming. Bugs often crawled into his throat at the orphanage, especially when he slept with his mouth open, but they never left a warm or welcoming feeling.

His father might have reached out to Bolt sooner— unless he lived too far away to send for his son. Unless, as a Baron, he had been too busy with Baron-like things, whatever they might be, to invite Bolt home.

Unless.

Unless.

Bolt sprang up like the broken springs on his seat. It was as if Bolt's new optimism fueled a hidden reservoir of bravery previously untapped, like a spigot run dry until the pipe is repaired. Which reminded Bolt that most of the bathtub pipes at the orphanage were broken, and he needed a bath.

Emboldened, Bolt no longer felt tethered to his seat. He would explore the train, perhaps find a bathroom where he could clean himself up. He would meet his new family soon. He needed to smell nice for them, look his best, and make a wonderful first impression.

He would not bolt, and perhaps he would never need to bolt again.

Bolt placed Penguin on his seat and strolled down the aisle. Boys with parents didn't need stuffed animals. He pushed open the sliding doors from his car. The cold and roaring winds whipped around him, and he considered returning to the warmth of his seat. Instead, still fueled by his newfound hope, Bolt entered the next train car. It was the same as the last—filled with rows of ripped-vinyl benches and empty of passengers. Bolt continued forward, through the doors and the momentary discomfort of freezing outside winds, and into a third car. It looked exactly like the other two.

"Traveling to Brugaria?" The voice was high-pitched and squeaky, but drenched in an eerie sourness. A man sat up ahead. A wisp of gray hair peeked over the back of his seat at the end of the car.

Bolt froze.

"Come closer."

Bolt approached, but slowly. He took a deep breath, reminding himself that he had a family now, and had no need to be afraid. *I am a thunderbolt! I am fierce!* he said to himself.

Bolt reached the end of the car. A thin man sat on the

bench, his skin clinging to his skull like a plastic film wrapping. He wore a conductor's hat and uniform, frayed and stained with blood, or maybe it was pizza sauce. Bolt didn't want to ask which, but he didn't see empty pizza boxes lying around.

"We don't get many visitors to Brugaria," said the man. His teeth were grayish black. "What brings you there?"

"Going to my new home," Bolt said, forcing himself not to bolt away.

"Then you should learn the Brugarian national anthem." The man sang, his high-pitched wail reminding Bolt of a cat scratching a dinner plate:

"We are Brugaria.
Brugaria are we.
We are—ARGGHH!"

After an awkward silence, Bolt blinked. "That's it?"

"The songwriter died in the middle of writing it, eaten by giant scorpions. That's the sort of thing that happens in Brugaria." The man coughed, phlegm soaring from his lips. "It's a horrible and dangerous place."

Bolt took a deep breath. He reminded himself that he would soon have a family. He was no longer unwanted. He was brave. "I'll be fine. I'm going to live with a Baron."

The conductor's eyes bulged. His vile breath hit Bolt's nose; it smelled like rancid corned beef. Bolt was familiar with the smell, as the orphanage served corned beef, often rancid, every other Thursday. The man's voice quaked. "Heed my warning—turn around. Go home, before it is too late."

From outside, a chorus of barks rang out, angry, loud, and violent. They seemed to collide inside Bolt's head, both frightening and familiar. It was as if a recurring dream, a nightmare he could not quite remember, had reawakened.

The conductor glanced out the window as the barks faded away. "Penguin barking. They are close. They are always close." His hands shook. His mouth twitched. "Beware the penguins."

"Beware the penguins?" Bolt imagined small, funny creatures with floppy, webbed feet. He thought of his stuffed animal. He rolled his eyes.

"Do not eye roll. Just beware!" The man leapt up, raised his hands, and howled, "Beware! Beware! Beware!"

Bolt screamed, turned, and bolted away. He no longer cared about feigned bravery. Behind him, the man continued to holler. "Beware Brugaria! Beware the always-full Brugarian moon! Beware the penguins!"

Bolt didn't stop running until he was through the next two cars and sitting back in his seat, clutching his one-winged stuffed penguin. His heart pounded in his chest.

Thumpa-thumpa-thumpa.

Mr. Smoof stirred and opened his eyes. Bolt wondered if his pounding heart had woken him. The assistant

headmaster blinked twice and then looked around in a mild panic as if he had forgotten where he was. But once he saw Bolt, he relaxed, and scowled. "Oh, yes. You. The train. Right." He checked his watch. "We must be almost there. Thankfully. It's impossible to sleep on these cars."

Bolt was about to point out that Mr. Smoof had been sleeping without any problems, but instead raised the more pressing concern. "Do you know why we should beware the penguins?"

"What are you talking about?" Mr. Smoof rubbed his chin and rolled his eyes.

"I heard the train conductor say it, and he also warned about eye rolling."

"You must have misheard," said Mr. Smoof, rolling his eyes again. "Perhaps he said, *Behind the pengoes.*"

"What does that mean?"

"How should I know? I'm not from Brugaria. We're in a strange country, so people act strangely. Otherwise they wouldn't call them strange countries, would they? Now, enough talking. Wake me when we arrive."

Mr. Smoof leaned back and his snoring commenced almost immediately. Bolt wished he could fall asleep, too. Instead, he looked out the window. Twisted tree limbs once again scratched against it, reaching out with their ice-tipped claws. The car jiggled.

Outside, barks rang out. Penguins? Bolt tried his best

to ignore them. But the words of the conductor stayed with him.

Beware the penguins.

Bolt hugged his stuffed animal despite being fully aware he was too old for such comforts, reminding himself he would soon be with his real family.

He tried to convince himself that his new life would be grand, despite the penguin barks chilling his spine with their terrorizing and nightmarish familiarity.

3.

Of Bushy Hair and Horns

The man on the train had said the Brugarian moon was always full. That seemed odd, if not impossible, but Bolt was thankful for it, as the bright globe splashed light—the only light—onto the vacant train station platform. A heavy mist covered the ground. Bolt could not see his shoes. He clutched his small bag so tightly, his fingers turned white.

Bolt didn't have much inside his bag—some socks, two pairs of underwear, an old toothbrush missing half its bristles, and his stuffed penguin, the latter hurriedly crammed inside when the train had stopped.

A small drab wooden sign on the platform read *Welcome to Volgelplatz.*

Actually, it read *elcome to Volgelplat.* The first and last letters were missing along with chunks of wood, as if something had chewed on the sign.

A light dusting of snow spread over the ground. Bolt wished he had a hat and mittens, but the boys at the Oak Wilt Home for Unwanted Boys were not given such luxuries. Once, Bolt had been given a pair of wool socks, but that was before they were devoured during what became known as "the Night of the Thousand Moths." Reporters had taken pictures of the unfortunate event, and Bolt's face had even made the papers, although it was hard to see much of his face due to the thick coat of angry moths that covered it.

A lone dirt road rambled along the side of the platform. It emerged from a dark forest, past the platform and a small, rustic cottage—the only building within sight—and then disappeared back into the woods.

Not even a streetlamp shone, although light flowed from the small cottage's downstairs windows, an oasis from the dark.

Mr. Smoof waved from the train. "This is where we part."

"A-aren't you coming with m-me?" asked Bolt, his voice shivering from both the cold and the idea of being alone. Bolt had no experience being alone. Even a grumpy companion who smelled like sausages was better than none at all.

Mr. Smoof shook his head. "I promised to accompany you to Brugaria. I have fulfilled my obligations."

"But you can't just leave me here."

"Of course I can. The train comes just once a month, and I have no intention of staying here for even one more second. A carriage should pick you up shortly. At least that's what I was told. You're a Volgelplatzian now. Or maybe a Volgelplatzer? Good luck, Humboldt Wattle." Barking erupted from far away. "You'll need it."

The train hurried forward, its wheels squealing over the rusting rails. Mr. Smoof disappeared back into the car. The train picked up speed rapidly, as if it were anxious to depart as quickly as possible. Black plumes of smog lingered in its wake, quickly blotting out the train.

Bolt fought the urge to rip open his bag and grab his stuffed penguin inside. He needed to be brave for his father.

Closing his eyes, Bolt imagined family beach vacations. He pictured a swing set in his backyard and picnics filled with family games of water polo.

Bolt wondered if families played water polo together; since he had never had a family, he didn't know.

As Bolt stood on the dark and chilly platform, he thought of the boys at the orphanage. Did they miss him? Were they envious he would soon be with his father? When they were adopted, would they play water polo?

And what would Bolt's father think of him? If he hoped Bolt would be cute or cuddly, like many of the other boys back at the orphanage, he would be disappointed. Unlike those boys, Bolt was untalented, too. Tenor could sing.

Scholar was smart—he knew all the state capitals, even both Dakotas. Pseudonym was clever, and was particularly good at coming up with nicknames for all the boys.

But Bolt's only talent was bolting from unfortunate circumstances. If he had another talent, he had not yet discovered it.

A twig cracked, and Bolt snapped open his eyes as something sprinted in the woods just past the platform, something small and quick.

A penguin stood near the tree line, staring back at Bolt, its eyes blazing red below stern, bushy eyebrows. Feet with orange webbing tapped on top of the snow-speckled ground. Tufts of white and black hair sprung out from its temples, and what looked like horns rose from its head.

As Bolt locked eyes with the creature, his head filled with frightening images. In his mind, Bolt could see penguins attacking humans. He saw penguins chasing cute bunny rabbits. He saw penguins burping without saying, "Excuse me." The images were disturbing and discombobulating.

It was as if Bolt could read the animal's thoughts, and those disturbing thoughts did not make for happy reading.

Grasping his bag tightly, Bolt rushed down the platform steps, nearly slipping on ice, and sprinted toward the glowing cottage. He did not look behind him. He could feel the penguin watching him, following him.

Beware the penguins!

Bolt reached the building's porch. Laughter and music streamed out into the street. He smelled chocolate chip cookies. Over the door was painted in white letters *The Dead Penguin Inn*, along with a painting of a grim and determined penguin. The picture did not look welcoming—in fact, quite the opposite—but someone had taped a piece of paper below the picture that read *All who seek protection are welcome inside.* Encouraged, Bolt swung open the heavy wooden door and stepped through the doorway.

The door slammed shut behind him.

A dozen pairs of eyes stared at Bolt. No one moved. No one breathed. The place was silent and it smelled of burnt toast.

From the back of the room, a woman emitted a loud, harrowing scream. Bolt, filled with terror, froze to the spot just inside the entryway of the building, like a tongue on a chilled lamppost.

4.
The Dead Penguin Inn

Bolt stood inside a large, rustic tavern, the woman's scream still bouncing off its walls. A fire burned in the hearth against the far wall, its flickering flames weakly lighting the room. A few lamps hung from the roof beams above.

The men wore lederhosen—classic Alpine leather breeches. To Bolt, the garments looked like shorts with suspenders. The women wore dirndls—dresses with laced bodices above the waists and white shirts with short, puffy sleeves underneath.

Their clothes reminded Bolt of images he had seen in a storybook long ago. Too bad that storybook had also been filled with pictures of trolls, horrid witches in candy houses, and people-eating ogres.

"Sorry about the screaming," said a woman in the back. "I just got a paper cut."

All the eyes in the room rested on Bolt. Each stare felt hostile and threatening. No one said a word as Bolt fidgeted in his too-small pants.

"I came inside because I thought I heard music," croaked Bolt. "And smelled cookies."

An old man stood up in the very back of the tavern, with skin as wrinkled as a raisin. "We have no cookies for you!" Under the man's suspenders was a shirt with a picture of a whale, its mouth open as if emitting a mighty and menacing scream. "Who are you?" he demanded. His voice cracked, as weathered as his skin.

"I'm no one," Bolt muttered, stepping back as if pushed by the man's unwelcoming stare. "I just got off the train."

"No one ever gets off that train," said the man, staring at Bolt. His eyes narrowed. He waved a large stick. No, not a stick. It was a loaf of bread. The man thwacked the bread on a table, knocking over three mugs of ale.

"Watch it, Günter!" cried the bartender, a large man with forearms bigger than Bolt's head. He yelled into the kitchen, "You're overbaking the French bread again, Boris. It's too crusty!"

"Sorry!" yelled a man from the kitchen.

When the boys had fought with one another at the orphanage, Bolt had often stepped in with a joke or a friendly comment. It would lighten the mood and they all would be friends again. "That's a whale of a shirt," he said to Günter, smiling.

The mood did not lighten. If anything, it darkened. Günter sneered. His lips trembled with fury. "You mock the whales?"

Bolt stepped back again, banging into the closed door behind him. "No. I have nothing against whales."

"You lie!" bellowed Günter.

"Calm down. The lad must be here for the festival," said a woman in the back, the same woman who had screamed from her paper cut. She seemed kind. She smiled and her bright rosy cheeks glowed. Other patrons smiled, too. The despair that had iced the room seemed to melt away. "Right? You're here for the festival?"

"If he is here for the festival, where is his beak?" demanded Günter, waving his French bread in the air.

Bolt scratched his head. "I don't have a beak. And what festival? I've never been to a festival before."

The paper-cut woman's smile vanished, and her rosy cheeks turned white. Despair re-iced the room like a snow cone machine.

"I knew it!" shouted Günter, pointing his bread at Bolt. "Why are you here, whale hater?"

"I don't hate whales. Truly." Bolt wondered if he might be safer bolting back to the train platform. But then he remembered the penguin lurking outside. No, it was safer here, even with a threatening man wielding a dangerous loaf of crusty bread.

Bolt stood straight. He was here for his family. His real family. The thought made him braver. He stuck his chin up. "I'm here to live with a Baron," he declared with a confident smile. The crowd gasped. Some people bit their fingernails, and other people bit their neighbor's fingernails. There was a lot of fingernail biting going on. Bolt's confidence ebbed. "Maybe you know him? Baron Chordata?"

The rosy-cheeked woman screamed. Three people fainted.

"He spoke the name of the cursed!" shouted Günter.

The bartender gripped a ceramic mug so tightly, the cup shattered in his hand. The broken pieces rained to the floor, but the bartender didn't seem to notice.

Bolt told himself that he was fierce and strong like a thunderbolt, and not like someone who wanted to bolt out of the room and hide under a bed.

Günter spun, jabbing his loaf of French bread and glaring at Bolt. "This boy is evil. I say we tie him up. Feed him to the alligators." He looked around the room. "Anyone have any alligators?" No one answered. Apparently, the room was alligator-less. "Well, we could feed him to something else, then."

"He's just a child," said the formerly rosy-cheeked woman. She was no longer screaming, but her cheeks remained ashen.

"Evil comes in all sizes," said Günter. "You all know that as well as I."

"I-I'm only an orphan," sputtered Bolt. "Or at least I was. But I'll soon be going on picnics and playing water polo with Baron Chordata. Families play water polo together, right?"

No one answered his question, for upon hearing the Baron's name, two more people screamed and one fainted.

"Don't say his name," hissed the bartender.

"He will eat you for dinner. Or maybe lunch!" warned a short man at a table near Bolt. "Or breakfast. I always find a big breakfast is important."

The crowd murmured in agreement.

"Stop scaring the child," said the bartender. "No one knows if the Baron eats children. Not live ones, anyway."

I'm not scared, I'm fierce, Bolt said to himself with as much fierceness as he could muster, which was very little. Surely the Baron could not be as bad as everyone seemed to think.

"I say we tie this whale hater up! Make him talk!" howled the bread-waving Günter.

"I really don't hate whales," Bolt said.

"Leave the child alone," said the bartender. He spoke in a loud and forceful tone. "It's late, Günter. You should call it a night."

"But he is in league with the devil, I tell you!" The man hoisted the bread over his head, narrowly missing

smashing a lantern that hung from the ceiling by an iron chain.

"Stop living in the past," growled the bartender. "All you whale folk live in the past."

"The times are changing," roared the old man. "Or rather, going back to how they were, so you could say times changed and are now reverting. But the Brotherhood is the sworn protector of Brugaria. It is needed now, more than ever."

"Go home," growled the bartender, pointing to the door. To the crowd he shouted, "And the rest of you, go back to your business. Free grog on the house."

The patrons cheered, the promise of free grog shaking their interest in everything else. As Günter walked toward the door, he grunted and stared at the orphan, his eyes slits of menace. "I'll be watching you, mark my words." Before leaving he stopped twice to give Bolt an evil eye and wiggle his loaf of bread. "Whale hater," he mumbled, and slammed the door behind him.

"I don't hate whales!" Bolt called out, but the man was already gone.

While the patrons resumed their previous conversations, the bartender waved Bolt over to the bar. "Stay away from Günter if you know what's good for you," warned the burly barkeep. "But do you speak the truth? Are you here to stay with the Baron?"

Bolt nodded. "Yes, Baron Chordata."

In the back of the room, two people screamed and fainted.

"Stop doing that. Remember, some things are better left unsaid. Such as 'Poor kid poured curd pulled cod' ten times fast, which almost no one can do."

Bolt tried to say the tongue twister, but only got as far as saying it twice before messing up. "That's hard. But why is everyone scared of . . . the Baron?"

The bartender did not answer the question. Instead, he pointed across the bar. "You are being beckoned."

There was a small table in a cobweb-cluttered corner of the room. Shadows and a dull haze hovered over someone sitting there wearing a gray, floppy, and pointy witch hat. The figure stared at Bolt with glowing green eyes, waving Bolt over with a dark, bony hand,

"I wouldn't keep her waiting if I were you," said the bartender. "The Fortune Teller does not like waiting."

Bolt trudged slowly toward the waving hand. "I'll be brave, for my father," he mumbled to himself. If not for that mumbling, he would have likely bolted out of the room and under a bed, as far away as possible.

Later, he would regret that he did not.

5.
The Fortune Teller's Warning

As Bolt approached the Fortune Teller, he heard music, as if from a wind chime. It sounded a bit like "Twinkle, Twinkle, Little Star," but a particularly spooky and off-key version of it.

A woman sat at the table with deep crevices on her forehead and sunken, bloodshot eyes. Wispy gray hair peeked out from her witch hat, which also had a dead, blackened rose sticking out from its side. Her long black dress, with lace and ribbons that looked like spiderwebs, might have been appropriate for marrying a goblin. Dozens of golden chains circled her neck, most holding charms such as small penguins, tiny ornate spice boxes, animal feet, and animal toes. One necklace held a long sharp white tooth.

The chains clanged against one another. That was the wind-chime-like music Bolt heard floating in the air.

"Sit," she ordered. Bolt did, and shifted uneasily in his too-tight pants. "I am the town fortune teller, Blazenda." She spoke with a thick, slightly German accent.

Bolt stared at her. "I've never met a fortune teller before."

"I thought every town had a fortune teller."

"Not where I come from."

"You must come from far away, then." Blazenda absentmindedly played with the white tooth hanging from her neck. "You are here to stay with the Baron?"

Bolt nodded. He almost spoke the Baron's name, but thought better of it.

The Fortune Teller grabbed Bolt's hands and squeezed. Bolt winced in pain from Blazenda's tight grip. "Now, pay attention. I have important things to say. Do not be distracted by my floppy hat, my melodic chains, or my outfit that might be appropriate for marrying a goblin." Bolt tried to yank his hands from the ice-cold grip of the Fortune Teller, but her grasp was like a vise. "Listen to me," hissed Blazenda while squeezing tighter. "You are in terrible danger."

"You're hurting my fingers," said Bolt, grimacing.

Blazenda did not relax her grip. She peered deeply into

Bolt's eyes. "Leave while you still can. Go back from where you came. Beware the penguins!" she howled.

Bolt blinked. "Wait. Pengoes or penguins?"

"Penguins. What's a pengoe?"

"Never mind."

The Fortune Teller cackled, but no one seemed to pay her any attention. The rest of the bar patrons were too wrapped up in their own conversations and free drinks to heed a cackling fortune teller. She cackled again, louder.

"Why are you cackling?"

"I'm a fortune teller. We cackle." She gasped, and stared at Bolt's neck and the birthmark on it. "The sign!"

Bolt tilted his head. "It's nothing. It looks like a bird, I know."

"Not a bird. It is a penguin! It is why you are here, as legend has foretold." She then recited a chant:

> *"When the moon is high, beware the mark,*
> *Where danger lurks and penguins bark.*
> *For you shall change, you shall transform,*
> *When penguin spirit inside is born."*

"What does that mean?" asked Bolt.

Blazenda cackled again.

Bolt fought to stop his shaking knees. *I am fierce! I am a thunderbolt!* He thought those words, but did not believe them. He trembled.

The Fortune Teller leaned in closer. "Your life is in peril. All our lives are in peril. Only you can save us from the Baron's evil. You are the chosen one."

"Chosen for what? Save you from what? I'm not brave or mighty, I'm just someone who bolts under beds. And why is everyone so afraid of Baron Chordata?"

Someone on the opposite side of the room screamed and fainted.

"Sorry," mumbled Bolt.

The Fortune Teller released her grip on Bolt's hands to his great relief, and clutched the animal-tooth necklace around her neck. "This may be your only chance. If you free yourself, you may free us all."

"What does that mean? I don't understand."

The door opened, and Blazenda looked up and hissed. The room grew quiet. Everyone stared at the newcomer.

He was tall, a giant of a man whose frame took up nearly the entire doorway. He wore a black overcoat over a black shirt, with black pants and, oddly, white high-top sneakers. Countless scars ran across his face, like lines traced into the earth. One eye blinked; the other seemed to be made of glass. A shudder of despair filled the room, as did the smell of raw fish. The man reeked of it. He lifted his hand and pointed a finger out, straight toward Bolt.

"Come with me, boy. But hurry. Your life dependsss on it." He dragged out the *s* so he sounded somewhat like a snake, only more slithery.

Bolt shook so much that his seat almost toppled over.

6.
Penguins Calling

Bolt sat at the Fortune Teller's side, his knees shaking and knocking together like maracas. Together with the Fortune Teller's clanging chains, it made a jaunty little tune, although no one danced.

"Go," hissed the Fortune Teller. "Find me in the Old and Seedy Part of Town if you survive, which doesn't seem very likely. But there is a chance. While you live, there is a chance for us all. Remember, you are chosen."

"You said that before, but what does it mean? What does any of this mean?"

Blazenda shook her head and said no more.

"Now. Hurry," grunted the giant by the front door.

With a loud gulp, Bolt stood and strode toward the

fish-smelling brute, one foot ready to race the opposite way. It made walking more difficult.

"Are you Baron Chordata?" Bolt asked the man as they stepped outside. Inside the tavern, two people screamed. Bolt heard two thumps, probably from people fainting.

"Me?" the man asked, the word coated with a thick layer of disgust. "I am merely hisss driver. Do I look like a monster to you?"

"Sort of," admitted Bolt.

Parked in front of the entrance was a carriage led by two horses, black as the blackest part of night and then blacker still, if such a black was possible. The powerful beasts stood at attention, silent except for loud breathing. Clouds of steam blew through the cold air from their nostrils.

A lone lantern flickered from the perch in the cab up front.

"You may call me the Fish Man," said the giant. He gestured to the carriage. "Our ride."

"Don't you have a car?" asked Bolt, eyeing the transportation warily.

"There are no carsss in Brugaria." The Fish Man stepped up on the footboard and into the driver's seat.

"How come?"

"Becaussse there are no gasss stationsss." A penguin bark rang out from deep within the dark forest. The giant quivered and his eyes widened. "We must go. The Baron will be upset if hisss new boy isss delayed. Or worssse."

Goose bumps climbed up Bolt's back like an army of leeches. Rather than sitting alone in the carriage in back, Bolt joined the Fish Man on the front bench. It felt safer. As soon as he sat, the horses sprang forward in a frenzied gallop. Bolt grabbed the side rails to keep from flying off. The carriage rambled across the dirt road and into the forest and its dismal darkness.

More penguin barking erupted from the woods, and the horses picked up the pace even more. Bolt could not see where they were going, or where they had been. He could just hear the scraping of branches against the back carriage and the horrid barking everywhere.

"Why such a rush?" asked Bolt, shouting over the din.

"We need to be back, safe, before midnight. There are many thingsss in the night. Thingsss we do not talk about."

"Like what?"

But sure enough, the Fish Man did not talk about them, just as he had warned. The horses continued racing forward.

The barks were everywhere.

Bolt could feel each one, almost as if penguins were sitting next to him. The sounds echoed inside his head, sounds of anger and, for one fleeting moment, a craving for fish sticks.

Bolt turned to the Fish Man. "Can you understand the penguins?"

The giant glanced at Bolt, his eyebrows arched. "What are you talking about?"

"Nothing. Never mind." Bolt touched the birthmark on his neck. It tingled.

The terrifying barks continued, and Bolt wanted the thoughts out of his head. But they remained, growing louder and more vicious as they banged around inside him like Ping-Pong balls sucked up by a vacuum cleaner.

Bolt reached for his bag and the stuffed penguin crammed within, hoping it might bring him a small bit of comfort, but stopped, reminding himself he must be brave. He was home now. His father was waiting. He would be strong. For him.

He wondered how the steeds knew where to go, with only the small slivers of moonlight to guide them. More barking erupted, a large cluster of yaps, closer now, and the horses trembled and fought against their bits.

Bolt took a deep breath. "Is it a long way?"

"Asss long asss the dead rot in their gravesss," bellowed the giant.

Bolt wasn't really sure how long that was, but it seemed far. He tried to stop shaking, but despite all his efforts, he only managed to keep his left pinkie still. The rest of him quaked in fear.

Bolt closed his eyes, wishing for the dark to turn to

light, the barking to turn to laughter, and the Fish Man to turn into someone a little less spooky.

When Bolt opened his eyes, none of those wishes had come true.

The horses stopped, rearing up on their hind legs with panicked neighing. Bolt clung on to the seat to keep from being thrown onto the road.

"Glub-glub," said the Fish Man, and the horses quieted. "Glub-glub." The horses steadied.

They stood on the path, unmoving and surrounded by the dark forest. The barking around them had ceased as well. The only sound was a slow breeze through the icy tree limbs, and the horses' panting.

"What's wrong? Why did we stop?" asked Bolt, grabbing the Fish Man's shoulder with trembling fingers.

The Fish Man pointed to the road. In front of them, a fallen tree lay on the path, blocking the way. There was no room to go around it.

The Fish Man peeled Bolt's fingers from his shoulder and stood up. "Wait here."

"I was planning to," Bolt said as the Fish Man jumped down from the carriage.

Bolt thought the obstacle on the road was too big to be moved, but the Fish Man wrapped his brawny arms around its branches and, with a loud grunt, slowly dragged the dead tree off to the side.

Bolt's sigh of relief was cut short when cold metal

pressed against the front of his neck. Someone had crept up on the carriage. He suspected the fallen tree had been a trap.

A girl's voice spoke. "If you utter a sound, I'll slit your throat."

Bolt gulped, loudly.

"I said not to make a sound, and that includes loud gulping," the girl hissed, her voice firm and cruel. She pressed her weapon against Bolt's skin, but not so hard as to draw blood. "I should slit your throat for that noisy gulp, but I'll give you a second chance. Just be thankful I'm the one kidnapping you. The other forest bandits would not be as merciful."

Bolt gulped again, but this time he gulped much more quietly.

7.
Robbers in the Night

Brutus was the largest and strongest of the Brugarian Forest Bandits, and so he had been chosen to cut down the large oak and drag it into the middle of the road. Annika had watched him, from her hiding spot in a nearby tree. None of the bandits knew she was there. She wasn't allowed to go on carriage robberies or kidnappings—her father strictly forbade it—but she was almost thirteen years old and that was quite old enough for bandit deeds, thank you very much.

She had followed the gang that night, quietly and carefully, hiding in the shadows. It hadn't been too difficult. Annika, after all, was the greatest bandit who ever lived.

Or, rather, Annika *would* be the greatest bandit who ever lived, someday. She just had to prove it by doing something bandit-like. She was ready. She had been training to be a bandit, in private, for as long as she could remember, throwing knives in her tent and speaking in front of a mirror in a firm, cruel voice.

But Annika knew that being the greatest bandit who ever lived took more than knife throwing and cruel-voice speaking. She needed to be tough. Fierce. And also honorable. The gang lived by the Code of the Bandit, and the code clearly mentioned the need to be honorable, right after paragraphs on toughness and fierceness. That's why bandits always kept their word, at least usually, and they seldom cheated at cards, unless they were losing. Also, they never littered.

Annika hid up in her tree for a long time, waiting for a carriage to approach and the bandits to rob it. She would learn so much! Her first robbery, and maybe—if she got lucky—even a kidnapping! But possibly the only thing more boring, and uncomfortable, than sitting in a tree waiting for a carriage to approach in order to rob it was sitting in a tree watching other people waiting for a carriage to approach in order to rob it.

Finally the other bandits had grown restless, climbed down from their trees, and trudged back toward camp.

But not Annika. She waited. She would rob a carriage, kidnap the occupants, and prove to everyone she could do this, all by herself.

Also her belt snagged on a branch, and by the time

she wiggled herself free, everyone had left. And then she heard a carriage approaching.

The carriage halted because of the tree in the road, and a large man, perhaps as large as Brutus, jumped off the front bench to move it. Meanwhile, a boy, who looked to be about the same age as Annika, sat alone in the seat. He was thin and maybe even shorter than Annika.

Annika pumped her fist. Her first kidnapping might be an easy one.

A moment later, after she bounded silently from her perch, she scrambled along the side of the carriage, up to the front, and snuck behind the boy, where she pressed her knife against his throat. He gulped. She grinned.

"What are you doing?" the large man in the road growled. It was a low, menacing growl. His face was scarred, and his manner powerful and frightening. He stepped toward the carriage.

"Don't take another step, large frightening man in the road," Annika said, firmly and cruelly. She took a deep breath. She was more nervous than she had ever been in her life, but a bandit never showed nerves. The Code of the Bandit clearly stated that a bandit should never appear nervous when kidnapping someone. There was an entire chapter about it. That was easier written than done, however. Still, when Annika spoke, she tried to keep her voice steady as the code suggested. "I'm kidnapping this boy. If you take another step closer, you'll be sorry. Or really, the boy will be sorry, since he'll be the one with a slit throat."

The giant of a man stopped. The boy quivered with fright, but otherwise did not move, although he silently gulped a few times.

"You do not know whom you are dealing with," hissed the man.

"You don't know whom *you* are dealing with," Annika hissed right back. She was rather proud of her cruel and firm hissing. "I am Annika, the fiercest bandit of them all." Just saying those words made her feel braver.

"If you're so fierce, how come I've never heard of you?" asked the frightening giant.

Annika sighed. "I'm just starting out. It takes time

to build a reputation, you know." She had slackened the grip on her weapon as she sighed, but now she tightened her hold and pressed it once again against the boy's neck. "But soon I'll be known as the fiercest bandit ever, just you wait. Step back. This boy comes with me."

"Are you all right, Bolt?" the giant man asked.

The boy, Bolt, didn't answer, no doubt too scared to make a noise. Annika smiled to herself. She was doing quite well.

A loud penguin bark erupted close by, to their left. Soon other barks joined and then, without warning, an enormous penguin emerged from the forest. Annika frowned. "Good evening," the penguin said, bowing. "Put the knife down, Annika."

Annika scowled but lowered her knife. It was not a penguin talking, but her father wearing an orange bill on his head—a disguise meant to surprise in the dark. He wore old and tattered lederhosen in drab black-and-white. That was the uniform of the Brugarian Forest Bandits.

With an angry growl, Annika jumped down from the carriage. Looking at her father's outfit only reminded her how much she hated wearing her own torn lederhosen.

"What do you think you're doing?" snapped her father.

"I was only robbing a carriage and kidnapping someone, Papa," whined Annika. She kicked the ground. "You never let me have any fun."

"How many times have I told you that you're too young to kidnap or rob anyone? What would your mother say?"

"I don't have a mother."

"Yes, but if you did, what would she say?" As he scolded her, Annika crossed her arms and spat on the ground. "You could have gotten hurt."

"I would have been fine. I have some tricks up my sleeve, you know. Want to see one?" She held out a deck of playing cards. "Pick a card, any card."

"Silence," said her father. "This is no time for games. You are in enough trouble as it is." Annika put the deck back in her pocket. Her father turned to the boy and the giant on the road. "I am Vigi Lambda, the leader of the Brugarian Forest Bandits." Penguin barking, which had subsided during the kidnapping, now echoed anew. Vigi Lambda stood rigid, worry sweeping across his brow. The look was fleeting. "I'm so sorry for the trouble, but as long as we've started, we might as well kidnap you. We make most of our money from ransoming kidnapping victims, you know. We also hold an annual bake sale."

"What if no one pays our ransom?" asked Bolt.

The bandit mimed a slit across his throat. The boy shivered and touched his neck where Annika's blade had pressed against his flesh.

"You are making a mistake," warned the giant man on the road. "If you know what'sss good for you, you will send usss on our way."

Vigi Lambda sneered. "Not another word from you." He pointed to the forest behind him. "And I'm quite aware what's good for me."

A rustle came from the forest, and a dozen forest bandits emerged, all wearing identical penguin caps. Some held rifles. They stood in the dark, hidden by the trees and the night.

One of the bandits, shorter and heavier than the others but with a surprising lightness to his step, trotted out from the darkness and approached Vigi Lambda. In the night, his dark skin made his face almost invisible except for the bright white of his eyes. He nodded to Annika.

"Felipe, we're in the middle of a kidnapping," Vigi snapped at the round bandit. "You know I hate it when you interrupt a kidnapping."

Felipe whispered into Vigi's ear. Annika couldn't hear much of what he said, only the words "danger," "death," and maybe "sponge cake." She might have misheard those last words.

Vigi turned back to the carriage. "If you're to be kidnapped, we must be quick." He clapped his hands. "Let's go. Lickety-split."

Penguin barking roared louder. Felipe whispered again into Vigi's ear. Again, Annika heard the words "danger" and "death." And maybe "prune danish."

"I know!" said Vigi.

"You do not want to kidnap usss," said the large man. "The boy isss property of the Baron."

"The Baron!" Worry flashed across the bandit's face. This time, his look of fear was not fleeting. "But this is not his regular carriage."

"That carriage isss in the shop. Thisss isss a rental."

Penguin barks again rang out, even louder and closer. Annika quivered, as did her father.

The boy who was seated in front of the carriage looked even more frightened. He covered his ears and rocked his head, as if trying to keep the sounds from burrowing inside it.

"Please accept my apologies for stopping you," said Vigi, bowing and taking a step toward the forest. "We meant no harm. Go, and may the penguins be merciful." To Annika he said, "And you're grounded."

"It's not fair," she complained, stomping her foot. As the giant-size man in the road climbed back aboard the carriage's driver's seat, Annika glared at her two would-be prisoners. She lifted her chin and spoke as firmly and as cruelly as she could. "You're lucky we're letting you go. But next time, you'd better watch out for Annika Lambda. The fiercest bandit of them all!"

"Very firm and cruel. Nicely done," remarked Felipe, but Vigi Lambda frowned.

The driver of the carriage shouted, "C'mon, you nagsss! Midnight loomsss!" He snapped the reins, and the horses sped forward. Barking rang again through the country-side as the carriage disappeared down the path.

"We should hurry back. The penguins sound like they are up to no good tonight," said Vigi Lambda. He turned to Annika. "And you! Sneaking around. Robbing carriages. Why do you do such things?"

"Because I'm the daughter of the head of the bandits?"

Her father harrumphed. "Harrumph," he said, and shook his head. "I'll deal with you when we get home."

"But I only wanted to—"

"Silence. We're having sponge cake for dessert. And prune danish. But none for you!"

Her head hanging low, Annika followed the bandits into the darkness beneath the concealing forest trees.

"I don't even like prune danish," she mumbled.

8.
Midnight Loomsss

After a few minutes of manic galloping, the carriage broke through the densely packed trees and into a wide and open meadow. The moon, bigger and brighter than a moon had the right to be, bathed them in light. They were high on a hill, and Bolt could see far off into the distance where powerful waves of a seemingly endless sea rumbled against rocks and crashed onto the shore. The water shone with a strange phosphorescent glow.

"The Blacker Sea," said the Fish Man. "Home to the penguinsss."

"I've heard of the Black Sea," said Bolt, remembering geography lessons at the orphanage.

"Our sea is blacker."

The barks were silent now. Here, out in the open, things did not seem as bleak as they had earlier. Bolt breathed a little easier.

The path forked ahead, with the main path continuing straight and winding along a series of cheerful grassy knolls, and a second, smaller path slithering back into the dark forest.

"We're going through the cheerful knolls, right?" asked Bolt.

"What do you think?" The Fish Man led the horses to the smaller and dreary trail, and they were soon inside the dense woods again.

Although the penguins were silent now, Bolt couldn't shake the feeling they were hiding, and watching.

The carriage continued on, traveling upon a seemingly invisible path that wove through a dense thicket of trees. Then it emerged into a clearing and the moon glowed upon Bolt and the Fish Man once again.

The horses clip-clopped toward an ancient manor that stood in the middle of a vast, open lawn. Dozens of tiny windows stared out from the mansion like small, threatening eyes. Chipped and cracking gray walls rose high. A crumbling battlement rimmed a tall and dark tower that emerged from the disturbing building.

The manor stood upon the lawn, as cheerful as a gray, festering wound. If ever a place was haunted, it was this one. Actually, Bolt thought ghosts would be too afraid to haunt it.

"You are home," said the giant.

"I was hoping you weren't going to say that."

On the crumbling roof sat a large wooden contraption. Bolt couldn't be sure what it was, but it looked like a—

"Is that a catapult?" Bolt asked.

"Yesss. Most homesss in Volgelplatz have them. Many are used at the festival. But the Baron hasss not launched hisss for a long time."

"Someone mentioned the festival at the tavern."

"The Day of the Penguin startsss in only three daysss—a day of rejoicing and celebration. People come from asss far away asss Walross-Stadt and Alabtrosdorf to dance and to honor the penguinsss."

"Sounds like fun. Maybe I can go," said Bolt, quietly to himself but with a small trace of excitement. How bad could a place be that held festivals?

"The Baron is more likely to yank each hair out of your head, one at a time, wait for them to grow back, and then yank them out again than to allow you to leave the manor and enjoy a festival."

"He w-wouldn't really do that, w-would h-he?" asked Bolt, his voice shaking.

"No. He would probably do far, far worssse."

Bolt shrank farther into his seat.

The horses stopped in front of the manor, and the driver pointed toward the door. "We are here. It isss late. Go. And remember, not everything isss asss it appearsss."

"What does that mean?"

"If something appearsss, it may not be what it isss."

"That's not very helpful."

The Fish Man shrugged.

As soon as Bolt stepped down from the bench, the giant tossed him his small bag and snapped the reins. The horses flew away in full gallop.

"Hey, wait!" cried Bolt, catching his travel bag. "You can't just leave me here alone!"

The Fish Man did not look back. The carriage soon disappeared into the woods. An owl flew high above the treetops.

"Whooo?" it asked.

"Just me," whispered Bolt. He looked up at the manor. "Here. My home."

If a bed had been visible, Bolt might have bolted under it. But bolting into the dark woods was not much of an option. Bolt reminded himself that he needed to be brave, that he was no longer a scared orphan boy. He had a father waiting on the other side of those cracked manor walls.

Bolt strode toward the door, whispering to himself,

"I am wanted. I have a family now. My father is Baron Chordata."

Somewhere in the distance someone screamed, and the thud that followed meant they had probably fainted.

Bolt bit his tongue to stop its shaking as he stood in front of the manor's front door.

9.
Chordata Manor

On the manor's door was a large, tarnished copper knocker in the shape of a penguin's head. It reminded Bolt of the penguin he had seen beside the train tracks. It had the same bushy eyebrows and horns. Bolt was both drawn to the knocker—he had an odd urge to caress its eyebrows—and terrified of it. His thoughts were interrupted by a series of clicks, clacks, and thuds from inside the manor. Bolt stiffened.

The door swung open.

An old woman stood in the doorframe. She was a little shorter than Bolt. Her wrinkled face had a dull greenish hue and was covered in warts. She wiped her hands on a dirty apron that might have once been white but was now multicolored with grease stains, worn over a simple dress the color of mud and the shape of a sack. She stomped her combat boots on the floor as she rasped, "I am Frau Farfenugen. Welcome to Chordata Manor. You must be Mr. Wattle."

"Call me Bolt." He gave an uncertain smile.

"Oh, lucky me. The lowly housekeeper gets to call the new boy by a nickname."

"Well, you don't have to, I guess," mumbled Bolt.

"So now I have permission to not call you by your nickname. Of course not, I'm just a lowly housekeeper. Why should I get to call you by your nickname? Put me in my place, didn't you?"

Bolt thought about making a joke to lighten the mood, but remembered how poorly his attempt at humor had worked at the tavern, and so instead said nothing.

Frau Farfenugen moved aside to allow Bolt to enter the house. As soon as he crossed the entryway, she slammed the door, locking all thirteen bolts and latches behind her. *Click. Clack. Clunk. Thud.*

"A lot of locks," said Bolt. "To keep danger out?"

"Or to keep it in," Frau Farfenugen wheezed.

She glared at Bolt with a look of mistrust, or maybe hate, or maybe indigestion. Or perhaps all three.

Bolt frowned as he stared at the gloom around him. The place smelled like dread, if dread had a smell.

He stood in an enormous foyer with a timbered ceiling rising three stories high. From it hung an iron chandelier, dark, rusty, and as big as a sedan. Although hundreds of lights were nestled in the chandelier's clawlike holders, the room was dim, as if a heavy fog kept the light from reaching the wooden floor.

The staircase in the back of the foyer, although tall and grand, rose up into a cloud of thick dust.

"Take off your coat," said the housekeeper. "Our home is your home. And for that, I am truly sorry."

A wooden coat rack carved to look like a crying penguin, with small hooks sticking out of its beak, stood next to the door. Bolt put his small bag on the ground and tried to unbutton his coat. His hands shook from nerves, which made the button difficult to grip. But he eventually succeeded.

Bolt thought, *If only I had bolted away earlier!*

Then he thought, *No, I am home now. I must be brave. For my father.*

"Are you tired?" asked the housekeeper.

"Yes. It was a long trip."

"Woe is you. I am sure traveling is more exhausting than cleaning an entire manor until your fingers bleed every day, like mine do. But I shouldn't complain. I'm just a lowly housekeeper, friendless and miserable, never to be loved." She looked away and wiped her cheek. Were those tears? Bolt couldn't be sure.

Bolt watched the woman for a moment, wondering why she was so miserable. Maybe she and Bolt could be friends. Perhaps Bolt could cheer her up.

"In case you were wondering, we will never be friends and you will never cheer me up," said the housekeeper. She stared at Bolt, her eyes scanning him until they rested on his neck. "The mark!"

Bolt leaned his head to the side to partly cover his birth-mark, as he often did. He tried to ignore Frau Farfenugen's continued glare, but it was hard since she pointed to his neck and kept mumbling, "The mark. The mark."

"It doesn't mean anything," muttered Bolt.

The housekeeper bowed her head. "Of course not. People are born with hideous penguin-shaped birthmarks all the time. It's as normal as your being born with ex-ploding ears."

"I wasn't born with exploding ears."

"Better that, than to have been born with your birthmark."

Bolt shifted uneasily while trying to keep his knees from their continued knocking. "So, will I meet the Baron tonight?" he asked, desperate to change the subject.

"No, and for that, be thankful. You won't have many other things to be thankful for, probably nothing else, ac-tually, so don't start getting used to being thankful for things. The Baron has business at night. Every night." She squeezed a wart on her cheek.

"Maybe tomorrow he and I will go on a picnic," said Bolt with a forced smile. "Or have an ice cream social. Or maybe even play water polo."

The housekeeper scowled. "The Baron doesn't play water polo. And you think he'll throw you an ice cream party? You have a better chance of being churned into ice cream yourself." Bolt waited for a smile, some indication Frau Farfenugen was joking, but none came. He tried to shake away images of being churned as the housekeeper grabbed his travel bag and marched toward the staircase. "Let me show you to your room."

Her combat boots clomped on the wooden floor. She walked bent over, so she seemed even shorter. Bolt followed. As they crossed the room, Bolt eyed a large portrait of a little man hanging above an unlit fireplace. He had a huge nose, so wide and long it reminded Bolt of a bird's beak. Two tufts of gray hair stood up on the sides of his head, giving the impression of horns. As Bolt walked across the floor, he felt as if the man's beady gray eyes followed him, watching. The man's mouth was twisted into what might have been an attempt at a smile, but failed miserably. The man had very bushy eyebrows.

"Who's that?" Bolt whispered, fearing the answer. *Please don't let it be Baron Chordata!*

"Baron Chordata," said Frau Farfenugen.

Someone far away screamed and, Bolt assumed, fainted.

Bolt groaned. "Th-that's who summoned me here?" His voice trembled nearly as much as his legs. He stepped back, as if the portrait might reach out and grab him.

"He? No, that man died long ago. We should be so lucky. Our master is his son. He's far worse."

Bolt tried to imagine someone more disturbing than the man in the portrait, but failed. He also noticed a second painting next to it, a much smaller painting, of a man in a chef's hat who appeared to be screaming in pain while caramel sauce was poured on his head. Bolt decided not to ask about that painting.

"The Baron collects art and other things far less pleasant," said Frau Farfenugen.

"Like what?"

"Misery, pain, and horror—and unfortunately he collects them in great abundance. Now, come. We must hurry. It is late."

Bolt followed the housekeeper. As they reached the first stair, Frau Farfenugen suddenly turned around and leaned into Bolt's face until their noses bumped. "Did the Fish Man drive you here?"

Bolt nodded.

Frau Farfenugen's eyes opened wide. "How is he? Is he well?" The sarcasm slid from her voice. "It's chilly. Did he wear a jacket? He does not always wear enough layers."

"He seemed warm enough, I suppose."

"Good, good." The housekeeper's shoulders slumped forward as she let out a sigh. Before Bolt could ask why she was so concerned, the housekeeper resumed climbing the stairs and snapped, "Now! Do not dawdle! You must be upstairs before midnight."

"What happens at midnight?"

"Nothing good. Now, stop talking and start hurrying."

Bolt glanced back at a grandfather clock against the wall. Tall and ornate, the clock's tarnished silver face and rusted iron hands revealed it was only a few minutes before twelve.

Bolt's heart raced, and exhaustion spread across his body. Being scared was tiring, and he had been scared for most of his trip. He only now realized how fast his heart had been pounding all this time.

As they ascended the staircase, each step creaked as if moaning in agony.

The stairs ended on the next floor, and they turned left, then entered another stairwell, narrow, steep, and winding, that grew narrower and steeper the higher it twisted. They climbed up and up, round and round, in ever-tighter circles. They were going to the top of the tower Bolt had seen from the yard.

Slam! Slam!

Above them, again:

Slam! Slam!

Bolt stopped and stepped back, wondering if he could bolt downstairs. But remembering the warnings about midnight, he took a deep breath and continued his staircase climb. The smacking crashes grew louder the higher they went. Frau Farfenugen seemed undisturbed by the banging.

Slam! Slam!

Finally, the stairs ended at a door. The slamming came from the other side, from Bolt's new room. The housekeeper turned the knob, threw open the door, switched on a light, and boldly stepped inside. Bolt expected a monster to jump out. He braced himself, ready to bolt.

PART TWO
The Transformation

10.

A Break in the Action

"Ah-choo!" I wiped my nose after a particularly forceful penguin-allergy sneeze. The penguin caretaker and I were the only people near the penguin exhibit. We were perhaps the only ones left in the entire St. Aves Zoo.

The night air grew chilly. I shivered.

"Should I stop telling my story?" asked the storyteller. He looked up at the sky, clouds sweeping in front of the rising full moon. "You seem scared."

"Me? Never."

"Then why are you chewing on your jacket sleeve?"

I spit out a few threads that had caught in my teeth. "For the fiber?" I ignored the man's disbelieving stare.

"The boy in your story—this Bolt Wattle. His adoption seems quite, well, irregular."

"And so it was," agreed the man. "I heard that after the orphanage closed, years ago now, the only evidence the boy had lived at Oak Wilt was a coffee-stained piece of paper found under the carpet in the orphanage attic, next to a receipt for a pearl necklace. It seems the boy's adoption had been, quite literally, swept under the rug."

The man looked away, lost in his thoughts. During the silence I glanced at the penguins. They watched us, leaning in, as if they were as eager to hear the story continued as I was. "I think I shall take the males for my zoo," I mumbled. Males were bigger, and easier to see from afar. Zoo visitors with poor eyesight would appreciate my thoughtfulness.

"They are a family. You should keep them together."

"They are birds," I reminded him.

The penguin caretaker sighed. "I have not yet finished my story. When I have, you may feel differently."

"Unlikely," I said, picking a few more jacket threads from my teeth. "Continue with your tale."

"Very well. But let's leave Bolt for a few minutes, and instead explore the history of the Brugarian Forest Bandits."

"History?" I scowled. "I hate history almost as much as I hate children's stories."

"Knowing history is important. They say history repeats itself."

"Nonsense," I said. "Can I buy your shoes?" I sneezed.

11.

The Story of Vigi Lambda

One day, many years before Bolt traveled to Brugaria, a young flutist named Milo sat in the hayfields with his beloved, Marcella. The boy loved to blow the lush melodies of traditional Brugarian folk songs like "She'll Be Coming 'round the Fjord When She Comes" and "One, Two, Buckle My Lederhosen" on his flute. As he played, the notes soared up the hills and into the hearts of all who heard.

Milo and Marcella had been secretly married. Marcella knew her parents would never approve. Her father played the violin, and the rivalry between flutists and violinists was just as fierce as it is today. Marcella knew her father's heart would be broken when he discovered she was wed.

Milo and Marcella did not notice the bandits riding up on their horses; the sweet, enchanting sounds of the flute obscured all other noise. By the time they heard them, it was too late to run.

"Do you know who I am?" roared the largest man of the group from his perch atop a great black stallion. The man had a scar across one eye and a sour look. His black-and-white penguin lederhosen were torn and his hair was filled with clods of dirt. But it was the rifle slung across his back that alarmed the young flutist and his new bride the most.

"I am Vigi Lambda, the famous bandit," said the scar-eyed man. "I demand you feed me and my men goat milk, steak, and wine."

"We are poor farmers," said Milo. "We have none of that. We have some lumpy oatmeal and an apple. We will gladly share them with you."

"You promised me the apple," said Marcella, pouting.

"I don't want your apple or your oatmeal," said the bandit. "But I will take your flute."

"No, not that!" wailed Milo. "Anything but that!"

Vigi Lambda kicked the lad in the chest, grabbed the flute, and rode off, hooting with laughter. Milo lay on the ground, weeping.

"Don't cry, my beloved," said Marcella. "I'll tell my father. He will help us."

"But he plays the violin."

"I know. But I'm his daughter."

"No," said Milo. "I couldn't bear you leaving me now. We still have the apple."

"An apple is not a flute," said Marcella wisely.

"It will have to do."

All day long Milo blew into the apple, but it failed to make a flutelike noise. He tried to pretend it didn't bother him, but he felt as if the ache in his heart would never heal. He stayed up half the night blowing into the apple. As a result, he slept in late.

When he awoke, Marcella was gone.

"My love!" he cried. "Where are you?"

She did not answer. Milo searched the woods, but found no trace of her. She owned only one shoe, so Milo knew she could not go far, at least not without stepping on a rock or something sharp. He waited for weeks, and then months, for her to return. She never did. Every day he worried about her, and her feet most of all.

"The bandits must have taken her," said Milo to himself. When you live alone in a hayfield for a long time, you often talk to yourself. "They probably play my flute to her."

Milo vowed revenge. He practiced swordsmanship and boxing and gunplay. He wrestled wolves, shot slingshots, and learned to waltz. He wasn't sure if waltzing would help him in a duel, but he left nothing to chance.

Four years passed until the boy, now a man, was ready.

With his slingshot, Milo could hit a worm from twenty paces with his eyes closed. He could wrestle wolves with one arm. He even mastered the Revolving Ronde, Progressive Twinkle, and Throwaway Oversway, which were all advanced waltzing steps.

If any worm attacks, wolf fights, or ballroom dancing broke out, he would be prepared.

Milo walked into the forest. He knew the robbers lived deep inside it because they had left behind a business card that read *Robbers. Address: Forest, deep inside.*

He brought his apple. It was now four years old and a bit moldy, but it might come in handy.

It was early morning when he entered the forest, and late afternoon by the time he found the bandits. He simply walked right into their campsite. There had been no guards or scouts, an oversight that surprised Milo. If he were in charge, there would always be a guard on duty.

Standing in the middle of their tents, Milo yelled out, "Where is Vigi Lambda? I have come for revenge!"

"Who are you?" spoke a deep, commanding voice. Vigi Lambda emerged from a tent, covered in dirt and grime. Goat milk stained his cheeks and crumbles of cheese crackers coated his beard. Milo was disgusted. If he were in charge, the men would take regular baths.

"I was a farm boy," Milo declared. "You stole my flute and my woman."

Vigi Lambda squinted. "Yes. I remember you now. I threw away the flute, and I don't have your woman."

"You lie!" cried Milo.

"I promise you I don't. The Code of the Bandit quite clearly says that I must always keep my word, or at least I must keep it most of the time. I'm also not allowed to cheat at cards unless I'm losing. But why are you here?"

Milo took a deep breath. "Vigi Lambda, I've come to fight you."

Vigi laughed, a spiteful laugh. Milo shook his head. If he were in charge, he would never laugh at threatening ex-flutists.

They were now surrounded by dozens of bandits who had emerged from their tents after hearing Milo's challenge. "I don't enjoy killing poor former flutists," said Vigi, still snickering at the sight of reedy Milo. "Go home and I'll let you live."

The other bandits laughed. "Yes, go home. You don't want to die."

"I could beat you," said Milo. "I've been practicing. I'm pretty good. I can even waltz."

The men guffawed. They had no interest in dancing.

"You have stolen my love," said Milo. "You have left me bitter and broken. I shall kill you."

"I find that doubtful. But if you do kill me, you will become the head of this clan of bandits. The Code of the Bandit, Section Eight, states that anyone who kills the current Vigi

Lambda in a fair fight will become the new leader and will also be called Vigi Lambda. By keeping the old name, we get to use the same stationery. That is our law."

"I was not aware of any of that, but I'm game."

Vigi held a dagger, but all Milo carried was his apple, still uneaten. Despite planning this challenge for years, he had accidentally left his gun, sword, and slingshot back at the farm. The two circled each other. Milo stepped forward with his left foot and then stepped forward with his other foot, sliding it to the right before setting it down. He shifted his weight to his right foot and put his feet together. He then mirrored the movements, backward. In his head he counted, *One-two-three. One-two-three.*

"What are you doing?" asked Vigi.

"Waltzing."

"Why are you waltzing? I thought you were joking about that."

As Milo stepped forward with his left foot again, Vigi lurched forward with his dagger. But Milo had already begun sliding to the right to complete his dance move and easily avoided the blade.

Vigi's lunge left him off balance. Milo stepped forward in seamless tempo with the music he softly hummed, and hurled his apple at his enemy.

It struck Vigi in the head, and the villain crumpled to the ground. The apple had hit the cranial nerve that causes instant death, just as Milo had planned.

"He's been ballroom danced to death!" cried one of the other bandits.

The young man who just a moment earlier had been called Milo strode forward, his hands on his hips. "According to the Code of the Bandit, I am now ruler of this clan. We shall move deeper into the forest and become even more ruthless and clever, but with guard duty and regular baths, and we will never laugh at flutists again. And I shall be known as the greatest Vigi Lambda that ever lived, at least until the next one comes along."

Milo, or rather Vigi, led the bandits to greater feats of banditry. The bandits, now better smelling because of their bathing, and safer because of regular guard duty, grew bolder. Soon, they were kidnapping one or two people a day, sometimes more. It was not always easy to kidnap so many people. The bandits had to build an extra-large kidnapping hut to keep their prisoners, and always needed plenty of snacks for them to eat, but it was a good life.

The new Vigi made it fun, too. Once he had all the bandits rob a carriage in their pajamas, and another time they had to kidnap someone using only a sock. Vigi always joined in. He never put any of his men at risk doing something he was not willing to do, too. His men loved him for it. And he loved his bandit clan back.

One day, the bandits snuck into a house in a nearby village. They had heard a baby had been born, and kidnapping babies was quite lucrative. New parents were usually quick to pay ransoms, and babies didn't eat too many snacks or take up too much room in the kidnapping hut.

Back at the bandits' camp, Vigi held the baby—a girl wrapped in freshly laundered swaddling clothes. He made funny faces and soft cooing sounds at the infant, but he was not happy. Between his fingers, Vigi held the ransom note he had forgotten to drop off.

"Give this ransom note to house number 919," said Vigi to Felipe, who was his right-hand man despite being left-handed. Vigi stared at the note. "Wait. Maybe we took this baby from house 616?" He turned the piece of paper upside down. He muttered a curse under his breath. "919. Yes, that must be it."

Felipe grabbed the ransom note and ran back to town.

And then Vigi waited.

The rules of kidnapping were quite simple and very strict. Ransom notes were left behind, and ransoms needed to be settled within twenty-four hours or the victim's throat would be cut. After waiting twenty-four hours for the girl's parents to pay, Vigi ignored protocol and waited another two hours. Nothing. Another two hours. Nothing. And then another two hours.

"Are you going to slit that baby's throat already?" asked Felipe. The man was shorter and rounder than the other bandits, and not much of a fighter, but he made a wonderful pumpkin strudel. It was always a big seller at the annual Forest Bandit Bake Sale.

Vigi Lambda sighed and held the blade above the baby's head. The infant looked up and drooled, but in a very delightful way. Vigi gripped the blade more tightly. The baby burped, but it was a very charming burp. Vigi pressed the blade against the baby's skin. The tot spit-up, but the spit-up was exceptionally adorable.

"I can't do it!" wailed Vigi, throwing the knife away, where it stuck into a tree. "Look how cute and cuddly this baby is!"

"It's covered in drool and spit-up," Felipe said with a deep frown, plugging his nose.

"But it's very cute and cuddly drool and spit-up." Felipe couldn't help but agree. Vigi smiled at the baby, and the baby smiled back. "I will keep the baby and raise it as my own."

"But the Code of the Bandit says only men can be members of the Brugarian Forest Bandits and no babies are allowed," said Felipe. "I think." The Code of the Bandit was eight hundred pages long and boring, so Felipe had never read it. Very few bandits had.

"Then we will add a new subsection, allowing for unclaimed baby girls to be raised as bandits." Vigi tickled his new daughter, who squealed and then spit up again. "We'll call her Annika. Now go make us a pumpkin strudel to celebrate."

12.
The Stroke of Midnight

Back at the manor, as Bolt and Frau Farfenugen stepped into the tower bedroom just before midnight, Bolt's mouth was open, about to scream, convinced horrid creatures would attack him. But he closed his mouth before any sound escaped. There was no monster inside the room, although a monster would have felt at home. Bolt followed the housekeeper through the doorway and into a large, round bedroom, as comfy and cheerful as a funeral home invaded by vampires.

Everything was gray, from the gray walls and wooden floor to the antique furniture covered in grayish dust. There was a bed, a full-length mirror next to the window, a closet on one wall, and a large bookcase along another, dingy and grayish. The bookshelf was missing chunks of wood, as if rats had gnawed on it, and its shelves were stuffed with massive ancient leather-bound books, gray from grime. The dull, gray bedspread had holes. There were even picture frames on the wall—but inside the frames were merely pictures of gray boxes painted on gray backgrounds.

The large bay window was open, allowing the cold wind to slam the gray shutters against the wall.

Slam! Slam!

Frau Farfenugen dropped Bolt's bag onto the mattress. Dust spewed into the air from the bed. The housekeeper walked to the flapping window and closed it. "I was airing out the room," she explained. "It's been many years since we've had a prisoner here."

"A prisoner?" gasped Bolt.

"I mean a guest, of course. If you have any troubles, just scream."

"And you'll come running?"

"Of course not. What could I do? Sometimes it feels better to scream when something is trying to eat you. Besides, you're so far up, no one would hear you anyway." She looked around the room as if searching for prying ears, and she spoke in a whisper, "Do not leave your room until morning. Do not let anything in your room. Do you understand me?"

"But why?" Bolt croaked.

The grandfather clock downstairs chimed, its clamorous chirps loud enough to be heard in the tower.

Frau Farfenugen yipped. "It is midnight. I must go, before the clock finishes its ring. We may never become friends, and you may never cheer me up, but if you listen to me, you just may survive. You probably won't, but you may, although I wouldn't get too optimistic about the chances, if I were you."

Frau Farfenugen hurried out, slamming the door behind her. Her boots clopped on the stairs, growing fainter as she wound her way farther down.

Bolt ran to the door, hoping to follow her, fearing being alone in this dismal gray room.

The door was locked. He wrestled with the doorknob, but it did not budge.

The grandfather clock completed its clangs. Almost immediately a penguin's bark rang in the distance. The sound crawled into the room and up Bolt's back. A multitude of penguins roared in response, seemingly from everywhere. They continued to shout, growing louder, more menacing, and more numerous. There were hundreds of barks, maybe thousands.

Bolt unzipped his bag, grabbed his stuffed penguin, and ran to his bed, eager to bolt beneath it. He knelt and rubbed his hand along the wooden floor, which felt cold and clammy and slightly sticky. Yuck. Bolt wiped his fingers on his pants and instead jumped atop his bed, lifted his gray bedspread, and scurried underneath, fully clothed, shaking and squeezing his stuffed penguin as tight as he could.

It might not have been as comforting as hiding under the bed, but it would have to do.

"You'll protect me. Right, Penguin?" he mumbled, hugging the animal tighter.

The barks! They echoed inside Bolt's head like bouncy balls. Each one ricocheted inside him, burying itself deeper. As before, he understood them:

Destroy! Attack! Eat fish sticks!

Bolt tried to keep the barks out of his head, but like the ravenous clothes-eating bugs back at the orphanage during the Night of the Thousand Moths, they refused to leave. Not only were the barks threatening, but they also seemed to talk directly to Bolt.

Bark, Bolt! Join us and bark!

Bolt cowered under his covers. He had no desire to bark.

Well, maybe he had a little desire, which was odd, because he had never felt the urge to bark before. Yet, something about the barking *did* seem enticing. It felt familiar, as if a bark had been sitting inside him for his entire life. At one point, Bolt opened his mouth, but then swallowed the bark that wanted to come out.

He swallowed repeatedly, hoping to tuck the yearning to bark back to wherever it had been hiding. All his swallowing did, however, was make him thirsty.

Still shaking and with his heart pounding, Bolt reminded himself that he needed to act fierce and thunderbolt-like. He told himself that things were better now, and that he finally had what he always desired. His father. His real family. He was wanted, at last.

Bolt's mind wandered to a poster he had once seen in a book, a poster of a criminal. The poster had read *Wanted, dead or alive*.

The image stayed in his head as he trembled under the hole-speckled blanket, clutching his stuffed animal, wondering if it might have been better to remain unwanted instead of finding his family in this accursed house.

13.
The Baron Cometh

The next morning, Bolt awoke from a night of terror. The bags under his eyes felt like they had melted permanently into his cheeks. During the night, Bolt had quaked under the blanket for hours as the penguin barking outside had grown increasingly frenzied. The sounds had filled his head like air into a balloon until he thought his brain might pop.

The voices spoke to him. They called to him. At times Bolt shivered and nearly screamed with panic. Other times, he felt as if he was carried away by a wave of familiar barks.

In his dreams, which came eventually amid continuous tossing and turning, the eyebrow-clad horned penguin from the train platform chased him. Bolt ran, or at least he tried to, but since it was a dream, he ran in place without actually moving forward, and the penguin reached out with its wing to grab him. It snapped its beak and growled. It cried out, "Bolt! Join me! Be one of us!"

When Bolt woke up, he was sweaty from his nightmares and from sleeping in his too-tight clothes. His stuffed penguin was wrinkled from squeezing so hard, and the rip, the one in place of the animal's missing wing, appeared slightly enlarged.

Sunlight streamed in from the window, making the room's grayness less depressing, although the room was still, in general, gray and depressing.

Bolt stepped groggily from the bed. He peeked out the window, expecting to see swarms of angry birds dashing across the countryside in wild packs. But there was no sign of them. The sun beat upon the spacious grounds, the lawn calm beneath a thin snowy veneer, as if the menace from the night before had been all in Bolt's imagination. He laughed to himself. Maybe it had been!

The house sat on high ground. Bolt could see for miles from the window, across the long forest all the way to the rocky shores of the Blacker Sea. The water glowed and stretched on endlessly.

The manor's antiquated catapult sat on the roof below the tower. Bolt wondered if it still worked and why the catapult was part of the Day of the Penguin festival. So many things about his new home were odd.

It would all feel normal once Bolt met his new father. He dropped Penguin and kicked it under his bed. A boy his age needing a stuffed animal? Ridiculous.

Bolt strode across the room and opened the closet. A dozen black tuxedo suits and ruffled white tuxedo shirts hung from hangers, along with clip-on bow ties. The only other clothes in the closet were a few pairs of black underwear, black socks, and glossy black dress shoes.

Perhaps Bolt would be attending daily balls. The life of a Baron must be grand, with extravagant parties. Frau Farfenugen might have said differently, but Bolt was convinced he would soon be attending ice cream socials, along with playing games of water polo.

Bolt threw his old, damp clothes into the corner of the closet and put on fresh clothes. The shirt was stiff, with lots and lots of buttons, and the tuxedo pants itched, but they fit him well—it was a joy to wear pants that weren't too tight. He slipped on a jacket. He even clipped on a bow tie.

He wanted to make a good impression for his father. Still, Bolt would ask the Baron if there were less formal clothes he could wear. His father would probably be happy to find jeans for Bolt.

Freshly dressed, Bolt walked toward his bookcase. Most of the books in the small Oak Wilt Home for Unwanted Boys library were how-to books, such as *How to Protect Yourself from Moth Attacks* and *How to Capture*

Toe-Nibbling Moles. The orphanage also had a few silly horror books, but Bolt hated silly horror books.

Bolt approached his shelf eagerly.

He frowned.

Every book was about penguins. An entire shelf was taken up by an encyclopedia set titled *Everything You Ever Wanted to Know About Penguins and More*—it was twenty-two volumes long, so Bolt felt the title was likely accurate. The shelves also included a book about penguin chick feet called *The Little Prints*, another entitled *One Fish, Two Fish, Red Fish, Blue Fish*, which went into great detail about proper penguin diets, and a handful of novels, such as *Huckleberry Fin*, *The Lord of the Wings*, and *Charlotte's Webbed Feet*.

Bolt sighed. He would ask the Baron about getting new books, too.

Bolt tried the doorknob. Someone must have unlocked it during the night, because it turned on the first try. He headed down the dark circular stairs. After twisting and turning endlessly, they led into the main house. Here the narrow, gothic windows bathed the floor with sunlight. Any lingering dust had settled overnight.

The creepy dimness of the night before was gone.

Bolt took a deep and hopeful sigh. He ignored the iron bars over the windows. He didn't stare at the pool of dried blood—or what might have been dried blood—on the floor. He looked away from the note on the baseboard, perhaps etched by someone's fingernails, that read *Help, it's going to eat me!* Instead, he concentrated on smiling. His father would expect his son to smile. Family reunions were joyous occasions.

As Bolt reached the second-floor landing, a voice rose from down below, a screeching and snapping voice without a hint of kindness. Bolt stopped in his tracks, his foot hanging above the next stair. He eyed the great hall below, where a small man in a black cape stood, his back to Bolt. Next to the cape-clad man stood Frau Farfenugen. The two were about the same height. The housekeeper trembled.

"What do you mean we have no flounder chips?" screamed the man. His voice was soaked in nastiness, like a rag dropped in kerosene, wrung out, and then dropped in again.

"I am sorry, sir. They were out of flounder chips. We had so many other treats, I thought you wouldn't mind."

"You thought? You are not here to think. You're a lowly housekeeper."

"So true, sir. Sorry, sir. Of course I won't ever think again. What was I thinking? Something, and that's not good at all. Not good for someone as lowly as me."

"Next time, when I say flounder chips, I want flounder chips! If you ignore my demands again, I shall feed your elbows to a pack of wild bears and dip your toes into a vat of boiling prune juice. Do you want your toes pruned?"

"No, sir. Never, sir."

"I should hope not. Do not disobey me again or I shall get very angry! And you don't want to see me very angry!"

Frau Farfenugen stared at the floor. She squeaked, "No, sir. It shall not happen again. Not from this lowly housekeeper."

Bolt stood at the top of the stairway, transfixed. No wonder the housekeeper was so miserable. Bolt wondered if it was too late to bolt, and whether he could find his way back to Oak Wilt, and then under a bed. Maybe he could swim across the Blacker Sea and convince Ms. Blackensmear he wasn't a purple pen running out of ink. While he thought this, Bolt's foot still hung in midair. He put it down, and the staircase emitted a loud, lengthy creak.

The little man whirled around. His eyes flashed scarlet, glowing like embers. His brow furrowed and his face contorted with rage.

But as soon as he saw Bolt, the anger dissolved. He smiled.

Bolt gasped.

The man below wasn't a man at all.

He was just a kid wearing a tuxedo exactly like the one Bolt wore, and no older than Bolt himself.

14.

Questions without Answers

The face of the boy standing in the great hall below was white, pure white, as if all the blood had drained from it long ago, or baby powder had been sprinkled on him and then smoothed down. In stark contrast, his hair was jet black, with small tufts pointing out, hornlike. He had a large pointy nose, and over his eyes sat two enormous eyebrows.

They were very bushy eyebrows. They reminded Bolt of the penguin by the train station platform, the penguin on the door knocker, and the penguin from his dream.

Silly thoughts.

"You must be Humboldt," said the boy, giving Bolt a friendly, dimpled smile. "Welcome to my home. I am Baron Chordata."

Somewhere, two people screamed, and Bolt assumed the *thump* was from someone fainting.

As Bolt walked down the stairs, his mind raced. *This* was Baron Chordata? Impossible. He must be the Baron's son. That would make him Bolt's new brother. A brother! Sure, his new brother seemed a little mean, even sort of evil. But a brother was still a brother, and that couldn't be all bad.

Bolt had a father and a brother and a housekeeper and who knew what else?

The stairs rattled and groaned as Bolt climbed down them.

"You really must fix those stairs," snapped Baron Chordata to Frau Farfenugen. "They make the manor sound as if it is haunted." To Bolt he said, "Of course my house is not haunted. There are no such things as ghosts."

"Of course not," agreed Bolt as he reached the bottom of the staircase.

"Or witches," added the Baron.

"No."

"Or unicorns, goat creatures, or sea serpents."

"Or mummies, goblins, or werewolves."

The Baron sniffed. "Says you."

Bolt waited for the young Baron to smile, but no smile came. Bolt squirmed.

Frau Farfenugen curtsied. "Please excuse me, but I must finish setting the table for breakfast, and then do my

chores until my hands bleed and I cannot move without agony, as always." She clicked her combat boots together and, without waiting for a response, clopped forward and exited the hall through a large wooden door.

The Baron's eyes remained fixed on Bolt, staring him up and down like a butcher examining a steer carcass. "Your nose is a bit small."

"I always thought my nose was sort of big," Bolt admitted.

"No, it could definitely be longer. And your hair stands up in strange ways, but not as strange as it possibly could." He pinched Bolt's hair as if examining it for grease or texture. "But we can work on those things. Do you have any talents, such as singing, memorizing state capitals, or creating interesting nicknames?"

"Um, well . . ." Bolt stammered. "Not really."

The Baron shrugged. "No matter. Perhaps you have talents you have not yet discovered. We shall see, Humboldt." He smiled.

Bolt waited for a laugh, or some indication the boy was teasing him, but no such sign followed. Bolt relaxed a little. "No one calls me Humboldt. You can call me Bolt."

"Excellent. I have a nickname, too. You can call me Baron or, if you prefer, The Baron. No need to bow when you say it. But I like Bolt. It's short, and that's always good.

It's easier to yell things. *Bolt, wake up!* Or, *Bolt, don't move or you will die a horrible death!* Not that I hope to say that. You can sleep in as late as you'd like."

The Baron smiled again, but it was not a pleasant smile. If anything, the expression was unnerving. It reminded Bolt of the time Mr. Smoof had found a dead rat in the bathroom at the orphanage. The assistant headmaster had worn that same unpleasant half smile while serving "mystery stew" for dinner that evening.

The Baron wasn't only unpleasant and unnerving, though. He was young and short and thin, much like Bolt, yet something about him felt powerful and fearless.

Bolt looked around the room for a sign of a grown-up, such as a large shoe or coffee stains. He had been waiting for this moment his entire life. He would soon meet his father. His real father.

It was odd there were no pictures of him, though. Bolt stared at the picture of the dead Baron over the fireplace. The dead Baron's eyes stared back at Bolt. Bolt didn't think he would ever get used to the painting.

"Where is your father?" he asked. "Or rather, *our* father?" It felt strange saying those words, but it also felt welcome.

"Father? We don't have a father, or any parent," snarled the Baron, folding his arms and scowling.

Bolt blinked. "We don't? But why?"

The Baron thumped his foot on the ground, and his mouth twisted into a cruel sneer. His eyes glowed red. As he spoke, his voice rose higher and higher in both pitch and volume. "I am Baron Chordata. I make my own rules. If I say we don't have a parent, then we don't have a parent. Don't mention it again or I will hang you from a flagpole by your armpit hairs and raise you up and down for a week!"

The Baron's body shook, and steam shot from his ears. Bolt stepped back in surprise.

Bolt had been so certain he would meet his real father that this news felt like someone had slapped him on the face with a brick, or perhaps with one of the orphanage's brick-like fruitcakes. He thought back to the mysterious way he had been claimed—leaving the orphanage without notice and traveling across the world in the middle of the night. Had this boy-Baron arranged it all?

"I don't understand," said Bolt. "Why am I here?"

The Baron stomped forward. He stood maybe an inch from Bolt, staring into his eyes, eyebrows curved down and jaw tight. "Stop asking questions, Bolt. I have only one rule in this house—don't ask questions!" The Baron's face still burned purple with anger. He curled his hands into fists. Bolt stepped back. "The next time you ask a question, I might get very angry. You do not want to see me very angry."

Bolt had no doubt that he did not want to see the Baron very angry. He had a million and one questions he wanted to ask. He swallowed them all.

The Baron twitched a few times, his eyelids fluttered, but then his red face turned back to its pure white state. The anger melted away like a Popsicle in a sauna.

He ran his finger across the side of Bolt's neck. "Yes. Good. Just as I thought."

Bolt tilted his head to the side, as he often did. "It's just an ugly birthmark."

The Baron bristled. "Ugly? No! Be proud. It marks you as special. Oh, Bolt. You do not realize yet how special you are. I have been looking for you for a long time. Too long."

"But you're just a kid."

The Baron laughed, an icy and cold laugh, so icy and cold that Bolt wished he were wearing a winter hat. "You'd be surprised."

A chill froze Bolt's hatless head. He remembered the Fish Man's words: *"Not everything isss asss it appearsss."* Those words seemed important, although Bolt was not sure why.

"Enough. Let us eat. I'm as hungry as a man-eating penguin." Bolt's mouth dropped. The Baron laughed. "It's just a Brugarian expression. Penguins prefer eating fish to humans. Most of the time, at least." The Baron led Bolt across the entryway. "Penguins have a rich history here, you know. The entire town was built on them. In fact, a fine layer of dead penguin blubber is built into the walls of this house. My cape is sewn from penguin feathers."

"It's a nice cape," muttered Bolt, managing to still his lips. They quivered with fear, just like the rest of him.

If the Baron noticed Bolt's nervousness, he did not show it.

The Baron rubbed his fingers against the fabric, nestled his nose against it, and inhaled deeply. "We will get you your own cape. Soon. After."

Bolt wondered, *After what?* But he knew better than to ask a question.

As they walked, Bolt stared at his feet, still wincing from the painful realization that his real family was not here. Why had he dared to hope? Why had he believed this home was truly his?

The warnings Bolt had heard the night before all flooded back. The threats he faced had not vanished with the rising of the sun.

If his father was out there, and his family, he would not find them inside this manor's cracking gray walls.

15.
BFFs

The Baron led Bolt into a grand dining room. The room had a reddish tint to it from dark, mahogany walls, a red oriental rug on the floor that was faded with age, and blood-red upholstery on the dining room chairs. Thick red drapes hung from the walls, but they didn't cover any windows, as if someone had thought of building windows in the room, changed their mind, but decided to put up drapes anyway. A large wooden table took up most of the floor space with chairs for twenty people, although place settings were set for only two, at the end. Bolt wondered if there had been a time when great parties were thrown here. He doubted any were held now, despite his and the boy-Baron's matching tuxedos.

Bolt's dreams of ice cream socials and water polo games had been ridiculous. He regretted his misguided hopes.

On the table sat a golden candelabra, and a dozen silver plates holding an assortment of foods. Seafood. The room stank from its smell.

As they came closer, Bolt saw one of the plates stacked with trout and lined with lemon wedges, a bowl filled with live goldfish, and a platter covered with marinated eel tails swimming in a thick red sauce. At least Bolt thought they were eel tails. It was hard to say for sure. Other plates were crammed with equally mysterious seafood dishes, although Bolt recognized sardines on one plate, and what appeared to be green octopus tentacles on another.

The Baron sat at the head of the table, and Bolt took the seat beside him. The Baron piled seafood onto his plate—a handful of this, a spoonful of that. Bolt watched, but did not take any food.

"What's the matter?" asked the Baron, noticing Bolt's hesitancy to join in on the feast. "Don't you like our breakfast?" The Baron plunged his hand into the goldfish bowl, grabbed a fish, and tossed it into his mouth. He swallowed the creature whole. "They are best eaten fresh," he explained, sliding the bowl closer to Bolt. "Try one."

Bolt fidgeted, but for once he did not fidget because

his pants were too tight. His tuxedo pants were practically the only thing comfortable about this entire situation.

"Eat one!" screamed the Baron, his eyes glowing red and his voice trembling. "I command you to eat! You do not want to see me—"

"—very angry," Bolt whispered to himself, and before the Baron could finish his sentence, Bolt dipped his hand into the water, grabbed a fish, and swallowed it.

The goldfish slid down Bolt's throat. It was quite tasty. Bolt licked his lips.

Soon, Bolt had filled his plate with various foods, including a large helping of eel tails. "It's delicious," he admitted.

"I'm so glad, Bolt. I knew you would like it. I just knew it."

Bolt had not realized how hungry he was. He had not eaten much the day before during his journey, and with each bite he craved more. He couldn't stop eating. He grabbed a handful of goldfish, which was not easy because they tended to squirm away, and downed three in one swallow.

"Watch this," said the Baron. He lifted a large trout fillet between his fingers. He flipped it into the air and opened his mouth. The trout somersaulted twice before entering the Baron's throat, sliding down without even a chew. "Now you try."

Bolt looked at the pile of trout uneasily. Swallowing a

fillet in one gulp seemed difficult. Surely he would choke. But the Baron stared at Bolt with such intensity that he felt he had no choice.

Grabbing the end of the trout, and with an uncertain smile, Bolt flipped it into the air. The fish turned once, twice, and then landed in Bolt's mouth.

It went down the hatch without even a hiccup.

The Baron applauded. "Wonderfully done! I knew you could do it. And you said you had no talents. Oh, we shall be BFFs. Forever!"

Bolt grinned. He had a talent. True, swallowing fish in one gulp was pretty lousy, talent-wise. But it was better than having no talent at all.

Maybe he could make a home of this place? It might not be the coziest home, but maybe Ms. Blackensmear had been right. Maybe purple pens almost out of ink couldn't be too choosy.

"So, what's this about a festival?" Bolt asked, the food fueling his courage. "I heard it starts soon. I'd love to go."

The Baron raised his eyebrows. "Did you just ask a question?"

"Sorry," said Bolt. He gulped. "It's just that, well, I've never been to a festival before. I thought it would be nice to meet people in town."

"Nice? Meet people? The town is filled with villagers!" The Baron's face turned violet. Bolt cringed as the Baron

crashed his fist down on the table. The silverware and platters rattled. "The townspeople are common. Vulgar. We are above their kind. You will not talk to them. You will not meet them. Do you understand? I have but one rule. Never to mix with the villagers! One rule!"

Bolt's jaw dropped open and he leaned back. "Sure. Sorry. But . . ."

"Yes?"

"I thought not asking questions was the only rule."

"Fine. Two rules. You shall never mention anything that might break my rules again."

"But . . ."

"Never!" The Baron's eyes blazed red, and the tufts of hair that sprung out of his head looked more hornlike than ever. It took all of Bolt's willpower not to bolt under the table.

His next question, about picnics and water polo, went unspoken.

But then the Baron laughed and, as suddenly as it had erupted, his anger subsided. The Baron smiled, showing his dimples. "Forgive me. I hate to argue. Besides, I have something far better than the festival to amuse you." He stood and pushed in his chair.

Bolt followed the Baron out of the dining room, careful not to do anything that might accidentally disturb his new guardian.

He could not stay, not for anything in the world. He would yet be united with his real family—he could sense it. They were out there. Bolt just needed to find them.

Any other future was something Bolt refused to swallow.

16.
Fun and Games

"This is it," said the Baron with an extravagant wave of his arms. "What do you think?"

Bolt stood at the door of a large game room. Disco balls flung sparkles on the ceiling as they spun, the flashing lights dancing along mirrored walls. Colors bounced everywhere. Music hummed from hidden speakers, a continuous drone of guitars, along with a haunting organ and maybe an accordion. Arcade and vending machines were packed tightly together and included a Skee-Ball alley and a snack dispenser loaded with treats. Bolt wanted to try everything at once. There were no games at the Oak Wilt Home for Unwanted Boys, video or otherwise. He had only heard about such things from other boys.

"This is yours?" he sputtered, surprised, his eyes glazed from the lights and sounds.

"Was that a question?" asked the Baron.

"I mean to say—this is yours!"

"Better," replied the Baron with a satisfied smirk. "But no. It's *yours*. I had this made just for you. I have only one regret: the snack machine doesn't have flounder chips."

"I don't mind," said Bolt, although flounder chips sounded tasty. Bolt ran into the room. His eyes blinked at the blasts of light saturating the walls. He pressed a button on the snack machine, and a chocolate-covered halibut bar fell out. Bolt greedily shredded its wrapper and plunged the confection into his mouth. It barely stayed there long enough for him to taste it, but what little he savored was beyond delightful.

Without pausing for breath, Bolt stepped over to a video game with small birds on the screen—they might have been crudely animated penguins—shooting spaceships. The game leapt to life at his touch. Blasters blasted and stars exploded. Around him, machines beeped, tooted, and roared.

The Baron placed his hand on Bolt's shoulder, startling him. Somehow, in the few minutes he had played, Bolt had forgotten the Baron was next to him. It was as if all of Bolt's worries and despair had been blasted away, like the spaceships on the screens. Bolt blinked to clear his brain, but his mind felt lost in a fog, a heavy mist floating in his head. But he did not care. All he wanted was to play, play, play. And snack.

"Bolt, we are BFFs now," said the Baron, his tone gentle, like a wet cotton swab carefully poking a scab. "I want you to be happy. After all, I expect you'll be here for a long time. A very, very long time."

For a moment, Bolt was distracted by the Baron's comment. But then the game before Bolt beeped, and the Baron's words were flushed out of his brain. Bolt forgot about the boys back at Oak Wilt, and evil penguins, and terrible warnings, and the Baron's temper. He forgot he was wearing a tuxedo. He forgot everything but the blips and beeps in front of him. Bolt only stopped playing to switch games, or cram his mouth with a mackerel-flavored macaroon or chocolate guppy worm.

It was almost too good to be true. What had Ms. Blackensmear said about things that were too good to be true? Bolt couldn't remember, but who cared?

He had a vague concept of time passing. At one point, Bolt realized he hadn't blinked in over an hour. He shrugged, and still didn't blink. He didn't want to waste time blinking, not with so many aliens to blast and fish treats demanding to be swallowed.

The Baron leaned closely into Bolt. How long had he been there? Baron Chordata's mouth rested only inches from Bolt's neck, as if he was contemplating biting it. Bolt didn't flinch. Bite away! He couldn't stop playing the game before him, not with so many zombies surrounding his penguin army soldier. "Isn't this wonderful?" the Baron whispered. "Would you like to stay here forever? Just say it, and you shall."

"Uh-huh." But Bolt was too busy mauling monsters to listen carefully.

"Good," said the Baron, his voice flowing like a soft, soothing lullaby. "That can gladly be arranged."

"Sure, whatever," said Bolt, blasting a sea lion.

"Just think," the Baron said slowly, deliberately, into Bolt's ear. "A lifetime of playing video games. A lifetime as BFFs. And all you have to give up is something so minor, I hate to even mention it."

"Great," said Bolt, splattering a sea lion on the screen.

"You merely have to give up your human life."

"Yes!" screamed Bolt, detonating a minefield and completely annihilating an army of albatrosses.

"So you agree to my terms?" asked the Baron. "Say it. You must say it of your own volition."

"BFFs, forever. Got it," said Bolt blankly. "Whatever you want."

"I'm so glad we have an understanding." The Baron stepped back.

Bolt couldn't be bothered to reply. He disintegrated a dozen krill on his screen.

"Play, Bolt, play. All day and into the night. I will call for you when it is time."

Later, Bolt would revisit that conversation in his mind dozens of times, wishing he had paid more attention to the Baron's words. Instead, he moved on to the next game, and the next. His thumb hurt. His misty brain grew more mystified. He was in heaven, although a scattered, increasingly confused heaven.

"You should turn in. It is late." Frau Farfenugen's voice rasped from the doorway, shattering Bolt's concentration. He looked over to her, momentarily confused.

"What?"

"It is almost midnight."

"Impossible," said Bolt. "I just got here." He looked around. The one small window showed the darkness outside. The Baron was no longer in the room. Bolt couldn't remember when he had left. Several dozen candy fish wrappers lay by Bolt's feet. His stomach felt queasy, although he hadn't realized it until now.

He stopped playing but couldn't remove the game images from his head. Enemy creatures continued to fall, blasted, in his brain.

"You must hurry and go upstairs," groaned Frau Farfenugen.

Bolt looked around the room, trying to get his bearings. "I think the Baron said he would come for me."

"Do not fall into his trap. You must be in your room at midnight. You must!"

"But why?"

"Or stay here. I'm just a lowly housekeeper. What do I know? If your body is torn apart by man-eating penguins, then I guess I can say I told you so, not that you would be alive to hear me say it."

Bolt frowned. He wanted to play forever. He was the Baron's BFF, and Frau Farfenugen *was* just a lowly housekeeper. She hadn't even bought flounder chips!

A solitary penguin bark from outside the manor blared over the haunting organ and accordion music that rang from the speakers.

Those mad birds were out in the wild, lurking.

Bolt's mind pushed through the video game flurry still swirling in his head, like a snowplow pushing aside the drifts after a blizzard. He should stay. No, he should go. No, he should stay. The snowdrifts kept falling back into the path.

"Hurry. Come," pleaded Frau Farfenugen.

Bolt blinked, something he had not done for hours. His thumb ached. His stomach bubbled. "OK," he said, but it took all his willpower to mumble those two short syllables.

As he followed the housekeeper out of the room, Bolt did not think about the promises he had made to the Baron earlier that day. If he had, he would not have walked so slowly. He would have raced to his room as fast as he could, barricaded the door, bolted under the bed, and refused to ever come out again.

17.
Nighttime Barking

olt lay in bed. A long black nightshirt had been waiting for him on top of his bedcover when he entered his tower room. Before putting on the shirt, Bolt glanced under his bed. Penguin remained where he'd flung it. Bolt left his stuffed animal there, despite his yearning to grab it. He also fought the urge to hide under his bed, remembering the floor was cold and sticky.

Instead, Bolt lay under his sheets, his thumbs twitching as if still pushing video game buttons. His eyes wouldn't stop darting back and forth, lights flashing in his head and game sounds humming in his ears. He couldn't shake the mist that had settled inside him.

All his mist-shaking did was make the springs in his bed creak.

The clock chimed midnight, and almost immediately a din of cacophonous barking erupted from outside.

Bolt rose and went to the window, slowly, drawn to the night like a moth to a flame. Of course, flame-attracted moths usually catch fire and die. For example, the Night of the Thousand Moths had ended with a large moth bonfire. But the image of fire-burning moths floated away almost as soon as Bolt pictured it.

Bolt looked outside and shivered, but put on a brave smile. Beware penguins! What was he thinking? He shouldn't let superstitions frighten him. He had a home. A BFF. Shouldn't he be satisfied with that?

The barks were tinged with anger, but also confusion. Bolt could sense the penguins' feelings—hostile, yet fearful. Some wanted to attack. Some wanted to go home. Many wanted to eat fish sticks.

It was too dark to see anything from the tower window, but then the moon emerged from a cloud, its light illuminating the forest and the land. In the distance, the Blacker Sea glistened with its phosphorescent glow.

And everywhere, there were penguins.

Barking, angry, they cavorted across the countryside in packs. Some were gathered far away, near the water, looking for food. But many more roamed the lawn below. They pushed each other and snapped their beaks. They waddled across the yard with surprising speed.

Bolt watched in awe and terror. He told himself he was

safe up here in the tower, far above the penguins, but he did not feel safe.

One penguin, near the end of the manor's spacious lawn, caught Bolt's eye. It was bigger than the others. Stronger. Another penguin ran up to it, dropped a fish at its webbed feet, and then ran off. Other penguins did the same. Soon, there were dozens of fish on the ground next to this abnormally large creature.

The large penguin had bushy eyebrows and two small, curved horns on the top of its head. It was the penguin from the train tracks. Bolt felt its power, even from way up in the tower. The other penguins bowed to this beast. Bolt heard their thoughts.

Yes, master . . . We shall obey . . . Can we take a fish stick break soon?

The massive bird looked up to the tower and met Bolt's eyes. In that moment, despite the distance, Bolt felt the penguin wanted him. Its thoughts spoke loudest of all.

Come, Bolt. Join me.

The penguins outside, every one, all raised their voices in a prolonged yelp. A small, almost silent bark trembled from Bolt's lips, joining the chorus.

Come, Bolt. Come.

Bolt turned and raced to his bed. He yearned to dive under it, but remembered the floor was cold and sticky, so instead ducked under his covers. He put his hands over his

ears to keep out the horrible screams and commands echoing inside him.

But then, just as suddenly as his panic soared, the fog hovering in his brain stifled it. The penguin barks no longer felt threatening. They felt welcoming.

Join us. Come to us.

"I'm coming," Bolt answered. His eyes lost focus. He heard only the barks. "I will join you."

18.

The Night of the Penguin

Bolt opened the door to his room and climbed down the stairs, his mind nearly blank. Every bark propelled him forward, as if he were a video game character and the penguins were at the controls.

When he reached the front door, Bolt unlatched all thirteen locks. He stepped out into the cold night. His bare feet trod upon the snow-and-ice-spotted grass. But he felt nothing except for the desire to follow the barks.

The mist that filled his brain grew thicker.

It was a chilly night. The cold wind swirled around Bolt. Snow fell, large flakes that glowed from the full moon overhead. Bolt barely noticed them. The yard was empty. The penguins were gone, or hiding.

Bolt reached the end of the long yard and continued

walking into the forest. He had no choice. The words called to him:

Come . . . Join us . . . Fish sticks . . . Who keeps thinking about fish sticks? . . . Me, sorry . . .

Bolt plunged deep into the woods, toward the sounds. His face brushed against a branch and it scratched his forehead. He barely felt it, as the penguin controls continued to push him onward through the dark forest.

Then silence. The barking ceased. The moon shone brightly through a gap in the treetops. Bolt's mind cleared.

What was he doing? His face stung from the branches' cuts and scratches. His shoeless feet were numb from the ice. He shivered. He wasn't even wearing a coat—merely a nightshirt. Had he gone mad?

Two dozen penguins stood among the trees ahead of him. They watched Bolt, waiting for something, or someone. They swayed back and forth, shuffling from one foot to the other. Rocking, rocking. Their webbing softly plopped in the thin snow.

"Hey," said Bolt meekly. "You guys aren't going to hurt me, right?"

One lone bark rang out, jarring and fierce, and the penguins turned as one. From within the shadows strode the absurdly large penguin, their leader, with its bushy eyebrows and twin horns.

The beast opened its large, warped beak. A scratchy

121

and hideous shriek rang out, mostly birdlike but also, oddly, human.

"BFFs!" it roared.

And then it charged.

Bolt ran. He could hear the beast crashing through the branches behind him. More branches scratched and pulled at Bolt, clawing his clothes and his hair. His nightshirt ripped a dozen times from thorns.

The beast neared. The other penguins barked, too, taunting Bolt, following their leader.

Bolt broke through the tree line and into the yard surrounding Chordata Manor. He panted. His bare toes stung from the icy cold. Bolt looked over his shoulder. The devilish creature was now on its belly, skidding across the snow-speckled lawn. Behind him the other penguins did the same, a horde of violent birds sliding closer. Bolt kept sprinting.

A hundred yards or so from the manor, Bolt felt a large, heavy rubbery lump smash into his legs. He fell.

The beast slapped Bolt in the head with one of its wings. Bolt grew dizzy. The monster's mouth curved open.

Fangs. Oh man, it had fangs.

"I could get fish sticks for you," mumbled Bolt in desperation.

Bolt swore the monster chuckled right before sinking its open beak into Bolt's neck.

Bolt lost consciousness.

19.
Awakenings

Bolt wasn't dead, or at least he didn't think so. It seemed unlikely. He expected death to be blacker, or filled with harps. There was light. He didn't hear any music.

It took Bolt a few seconds to realize where he was. His eyes focused and his ears cleared. He felt the layers of dust in his nose, the creepiness in the air, and saw the bare gray walls around him. He was in the tower, back in his bed. What had happened?

A penguin had attacked him.

But not just any penguin. It had been the Baron. Bolt was sure of it.

How was that possible?

Bolt was wearing a new nightshirt, one that was dry and not torn. He jerked his hand up and felt his neck, where the penguin had sunk its teeth, right on his birthmark. A thick bandage covered the wound. Now that Bolt remembered his injury, it itched worse than a million mosquito bites. He grabbed the bandage, ready to rip it off and scratch his neck and scratch and scratch, possibly for weeks.

"I would leave it alone. It will heal sooner than you think." The Baron sat on a chair near the window. Bolt hadn't noticed him in the corner. "Sorry if I startled you. I was just brooding. It kills the time. With practice, you will brood, too."

"You attacked me! You weren't you!" screamed Bolt, inching backward on the bed, away from the Baron, although he wasn't all that close to Bolt.

"Oh? If I wasn't me, who was I?" The Baron stood from his chair.

"You were some sort of penguin. I saw you. With your giant eyebrows and your hideous bark."

"How is that possible? I'm curious. Tell me." He laughed, and a bemused expression crossed his face.

"You had a beak . . . and wings and . . . I don't know." Bolt felt foolish for saying it. It was impossible, of course. Still, it seemed true.

Bolt wasn't sure of anything at that moment. He needed to get away, if only to think.

His brain felt as murky as the air in the tower.

But first, Bolt needed to stand up. He swung his feet over the side of his bed and put weight on his legs. The room spun. His head felt like it was sinking in mud. He sat back down to keep from passing out.

"I'm afraid you aren't going anywhere quite yet. Lie down and relax," said the Baron. When Bolt didn't move, the Baron narrowed his eyes, and his face reddened. "I said *lie*. Do not make me say it again," he snarled. "Or I shall get very angry."

Bolt lay down. The Baron's face resumed its natural ghostly white shade. "That's better. I only have one rule. That you lie down to recuperate."

"I thought there was also an 'ask no questions' rule and a 'no festival' rule."

"OK, three rules. But you do not want to break them." The Baron crossed the room and approached the bookshelf. He lifted a platter resting on top of it. As he carried it closer, Bolt's nostrils filled with the strong scent of raw fish. "I brought you breakfast."

The platter was covered with whole raw fish, in all shapes and sizes, as if plucked fresh from the sea. There were large fish and small fish in different colors. The stench was overwhelming.

And so delicious!

Bolt raised his hand to grab a red fish, and then

brought his hand down just as quickly. What was he doing?

"I need to leave. To think." Bolt tried to sit up again, but his head throbbed.

"You need to lie down. I wouldn't steer you wrong. After all, we're BFFs. Forever. Just like you wanted."

"L-like *I* wanted?" sputtered Bolt.

"We made an agreement, you and I. Remember? You agreed to the terms. We are the same now, Humboldt, or will be very soon."

"Never. You are a monster."

"Me? You wear the mark of the penguin on your neck, Bolt. You think you were born with that birthmark for no reason?"

"Well, yes."

The Baron smiled, but like most of his smiles, it was disturbing and creepy. "This is your destiny, Bolt. The metamorphosis has started. Together we will rule, side by side. The war will come!" The Baron pumped his fist.

"What metamorphosis? What war?" asked Bolt. His brain was still muddy, and the questions popped out without his thinking.

The Baron raised his eyebrows but, fortunately, did not get very angry. "You've had a rough night, so I'll ignore your rule breaking this once. You will know all. After."

"After what?"

The Baron shrugged and did not answer. "Questions, questions," he muttered. "Don't test my patience."

Bolt needed to get out. He needed to bolt! He struggled to stand, but once again his head fogged and he collapsed back down on the bed.

"You will be better soon, Bolt. Better than you ever imagined! But for now, you must sleep." The Baron stepped toward the door. "Until tonight."

"Tonight? What happens tonight?"

The Baron laughed, an evil chuckle, as he strutted across the room, stopping only to look back at Bolt and chuckle softly again. He closed the door behind him. The lock clicked into place.

Bolt forced himself to sit up, fighting through the dizziness. He couldn't stay. He needed to escape. But where could he go? Where was it safe? If only the orphanage wasn't so far away. If only his family, his real family, was here to save him.

Bolt grabbed the platter of raw fish that rested at the foot of his bed. He would escape as soon as he ate. He needed strength. He threw a fish into his mouth and spat out the bones. He had never tasted better food. He ate another. He reached for a third, but pulled back. What was he doing? He was both eager to eat and appalled by what and how he was eating. He pushed the platter away.

Bolt would just stay in the tower for a few more seconds

to rest, and then get out. Just a minute. Or maybe five minutes. Fifteen minutes, tops. He felt so tired. He needed to sit for a short time, and that was all.

He closed his eyes. He only wanted to sleep. Well, he only wanted to eat the rest of the fish and to sleep, but sleep soon won the day.

20.
One of Us

When Bolt awoke, it was deep into the night. The light of the moon trickled in from the window. Bolt listened for noises and creaks, but the house was silent. He sat up, and the dizziness from before did not return. How long had he slept? Too long, that was for sure. He looked at the platter of fish still resting on his bed. He clawed through the rest of the food, devouring each morsel and spitting out bones. Every bite awakened some primal urge inside him to eat more. The bones piled up and up on the floor.

The fish gone, Bolt stood up, slowly. His head stayed clear. Bolt walked to the mirror and stared at his reflection. His face was ghostly white, and his eyes had a slightly yellowish tinge. His nose, already long, now seemed longer. His hair was always a mess, but now it appeared even messier, with two small tufts pointing up, like horns. He tried to smooth them down with his hand, wetting his fingers first, but his hair sprang back up.

His eyebrows seemed bushier, too.

His neck tickled and he tore off his bandage to scratch. He expected to see a gruesome scar. But his neck was smooth, completely healed. His birthmark stared back at him, undisturbed, although still disturbing. Was it even bigger than before? The wings of the penguin seemed longer and higher.

He rushed to the closet. He would get dressed and bolt. His real family must be waiting at the orphanage. Or somewhere. His family felt closer than ever, although Bolt didn't know why. He slipped on a pair of tuxedo pants and grabbed a shirt. He was only halfway through buttoning when he heard the grandfather clock's chime. One time, two times, and on and on until eleven.

No, until twelve. Bolt had miscounted.

Outside, the birds' howls rang out, but Bolt barely heard them. A surge of energy flowed through his veins.

He felt the sea call him. He had an urge to swim. He needed to bark. He would do anything to waddle.

His window lit up from the full moon up above. Bolt wandered to it, and the glow bathed Bolt in light.

His skin rippled.

Bolt staggered back, but the light of the moon remained

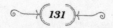

shining upon him. His bare feet grew, turning orange, and webbing spread between his toes.

Beware the moon! The more it shone, the more he changed.

A cloud shifted, blocking the moon's rays, and the transformation stopped, for a moment, but then the cloud passed, and the moon beamed its glow back into the tower. Bolt's belly expanded.

Bolt stared at his reflection in the mirror. His face morphed—twisting, elongating, his nose jutting out, turning into a beak.

Bolt staggered to the large bay window. He yanked it open. He needed fresh air. He needed fish sticks.

He opened his mouth to scream. Instead, he barked. His arms turned into small wings.

"I am one of you," he said to the penguins below, speaking in a whisper yet knowing they heard him.

Then, he felt nothing.

21.
A Nightmare Awake

In his dream, Bolt ran. Free. Powerful. He raced along the seashore with a hundred penguins—no, a thousand penguins—splashing against the tall, foamy waves. Fish flopped everywhere, and he ate and ate to feed an unquenchable hunger.

Drop one down your throat and move on to the next.

He was a part of them. A penguin. This was what family truly felt like. For the first time in his life, he felt wanted—without judgment, without worrying about being cute or cuddly, talented or not. He was wanted for who he was, for what he had become.

Bolt dreamed of barking on the rocks and diving underwater, swimming faster and holding his breath longer than he ever imagined before coming up for air and then diving back down. He had never swum before. The Oak Wilt Home for Unwanted Boys didn't have a swimming pool, or a river, or baths, or even large-size glasses of water. The water felt comfortable. Despite the frigid temperature, Bolt wasn't cold. In fact, the sea felt cozy, like a snuggly blanket.

He raced a shark. He danced with a skate and did the limbo with a squid. But then an orca appeared, a killer whale, and he fled, all his penguin brethren fled, fearing an enemy too big to fight.

Terror filled Bolt, an instinctual fear of killer whales even deeper than his fear of the orphanage's biting moles. But then, free from the water, the terror vanished and he raced through the forest, looking for mischief.

He and the penguins soon found it.

They surrounded two teenagers—a girl and a boy out for a midnight stroll, holding hands. They were skipping, smiling, whistling, until Bolt and his penguin crew encircled them. Then the teenagers shook and huddled together.

"Don't hurt us," begged the boy.

"We like penguins," whimpered the girl. "We're big fans."

Some of the penguins barked angrily. These birds felt no mercy, only a hunger for power and dastardly deeds. But other penguins hesitated, their brains addled, shifting among thoughts of power, and peace, and fish sticks.

Bolt understood them all.

As the couple trembled, hugging, a grotesquely large penguin emerged from the forest. This was the Baron, but now a penguin—of that Bolt had no doubt. The Baron-penguin barked, "We are penguins! We are meant to rule!"

To the couple, the sounds were merely the mad barking of a deranged and extra-large bushy-eyebrowed penguin, but Bolt understood the voice burrowing itself inside him like a worm into an apple.

The couple fled farther into the woods, but the beast followed them. Through the darkness, Bolt heard a commotion, and then a scream and then another scream. Moments later, the Baron-penguin returned with one of the boy's shoes.

Bolt sat upright, back in his bed. It was morning, and a cold breeze blew in from the open window. The bedspread was soaking wet, and snow had blown onto the floor, melting into small puddles. Wet penguin prints led from the closed tower door.

Bolt wore his nightshirt, but it was torn, shredded, and dripping with salt water. He exhaled, but despite the cold, no cloud formed from his breath. Oddly, he was not chilled.

A dead fish lay on his bed. Bolt picked it up and rubbed

his tongue down its side before tossing it down his throat. His arm smelled like fish, so he licked it, too. Both tasted salty, like the sea. He licked his own arm again, faster, rejoicing in the flavor until, appalled, he forced himself to stop, slobber dripping from his elbow.

Bolt stood and stared at himself in the mirror. He trembled as he saw his snow-white face and the two tufts of hair standing hornlike on top. His eyebrows were bushier—there was no doubting their new fullness.

No penguin wings sat on his sides; he had only human arms. No penguin beak protruded from his head. He was still himself, mostly.

But Bolt knew it had happened. It had not just been a dream.

Bolt had become a werepenguin.

The Baron had said they would rule, side by side. Bolt didn't want to rule. He just wanted to run, far away, and find his real family.

Family.

When he thought those words, Bolt's mind drifted to his scattered memories of the night before. Amid the horror and the revulsion for the monster he had become, he'd also felt a sense of belonging. He had been part of a family, of sorts. Sure, it was a terrifying family of birds that wanted to rule, enslave people, and follow the Baron's demented orders, but a family nonetheless.

Bolt shook his head. Ridiculous. His addled mind was

playing tricks on him. A group of penguins wasn't a family.

But what would Bolt's *real* family, the ones likely waiting back at the orphanage right then, think about Bolt's penguin transmutations? For Bolt knew, somehow, that he was doomed to transform again and again, every night, unless he did something. If he didn't stop his nightly mutations, if he couldn't, he would never be loved. He would never have a family.

As Bolt continued shaking his head, nearly overwhelmed with despair, he thought back to the Fortune Teller. She had said she could save Bolt. She'd said something about how freeing himself would free them all.

She might be his only chance.

In between her chain-rattling chiming and her disturbing cackling and her viselike grip, the Fortune Teller had also said Bolt was the chosen one.

She had never said what he was chosen for, but Bolt hoped he was chosen to escape his monstrous fate. He doubted he had been chosen to save anyone. That was the sort of thing brave and mighty people did, and Bolt wasn't brave or mighty, just desperate.

But Blazenda would help Bolt end his curse. She had to. He dreaded to think what might become of him if she didn't.

PART THREE

The Curse

22.
Another Break in the Action

Back at the St. Aves Zoo, the penguin caretaker paused. The zoo exhibit lights had been turned off and the full moon glowed above. The penguins in the exhibit were as silent as I was, watching our storyteller, hanging on his every word.

I spit out a large thread from my coat. I had eaten an entire jacket sleeve, and had started gnawing on the other one. "Never liked sleeves much," I mumbled, trying to deflect attention from my palpable fear.

The penguin caretaker nodded, too polite to mention the small hill of saliva-drenched fabric chunks covering the ground around my feet. "Perhaps I should stop the story now?"

"Are you at the end? You promised me free penguins at the end."

"No, I am not at the end," he admitted. "And I did not forget our bargain. The penguins are yours after my story, if you still want them."

"Of course I still want them. A ridiculous penguin story won't change my mind. Go on."

"I must warn you, we are getting into the scary part."

"I'm ready."

"I don't think anyone can ever be ready for what happens next." I stiffened, and the man looked away with a melancholy stare. "Let's revisit the Brugarian Forest Bandits. Perhaps hearing about them will lighten the mood."

"Hearing about violent, throat-slitting bandits who capture and kidnap innocent babies will lighten the mood?"

"Unfortunately for us, yes."

23.
The Runaway

After failing to kidnap Bolt or rob his carriage, Annika sat in her tent, stewing. It was a largish tent, big enough for a bed and a trunk with enough extra space to perform jumping jacks, if someone wanted to perform jumping jacks, which was not often. It stood at the outskirts of the bandit camp.

The camp itself wasn't much to look at—a cluster of large, foldable tents in a clearing in the middle of the Brugarian forest. In addition to a tent for each bandit, there was also a cooking pit, the kidnapping hut, and a crude bathroom that was little more than a hole in the ground. The smell from the hole-in-the-ground bathroom permeated the entire campsite despite 276 vanilla-scented air fresheners hanging on the trees, provided by an air freshener salesman in return for his kidnapped uncle. The salesman hadn't had enough cash on hand to pay the ransom.

But such was the life of a bandit—stinky smells, temporary housing in case you needed to pack up and move in the middle of the night, and questionable ransom-collection agreements.

Annika sat on her bed. Her father stood before her, arms crossed. Outside, Annika could hear the *thwick, thwick, thwick* of metal penetrating wood—the sound of morning knife-throwing practice.

"Let me join the men and practice knife throwing," Annika begged.

Vigi Lambda shook his head. "You know I don't allow that. You are not old enough."

"You treat me like I'm still a baby."

"You exaggerate. Oh, and I got you a new rattle." He tossed the toy on her bed. Annika glared at it.

"It's not fair," sighed Annika, crossing her arms. "I'm almost thirteen. How old were you when you started kidnapping?"

"Twenty-four."

"Well, everyone knows girls mature faster than boys." Her father frowned. "I won the bandit lock-picking contest last year. Remember? No one else even came close. And I'm fast. I can outrace everyone."

"Picking a lock and running cannot help you rob a carriage and kidnap its riders."

"But it can help me escape if I'm caught. Please, Papa. Give me a chance. I can be a terrific bandit—the best ever. I'm as fast and clever as a penguin!" Vigi Lambda bristled. Annika frowned at his reaction. "Why are you so scared of those birds, anyway? We have an agreement with the Baron, right? He protects us."

"We do!" her father said, although a bit too loudly, his brow furrowing. "But like glass hammers, agreements can be easily shattered."

Annika nodded, remembering the set of glass tools her father had bought a few years before. It had not lasted long. "The penguins are getting meaner, aren't they?" she asked. "More bold. More cunning. What if they attack us?"

"Nonsense," said her father. "That would never happen."

"But you just said—"

"I will not discuss it with you!" He stomped his foot on the ground. "I will not discuss it with anyone. I am the leader of this bandit clan, and only me. I can even show you my stationery if you don't believe me."

Annika buried her head in her hands. Her weeping was so loud and harsh, it made even the weeping willows outside the tent jealous. "You won't let me do anything. You won't tell me anything. You're not even my real father. I wish you had never kidnapped me at all!"

"Don't say that—"

"I hate you!"

Vigi Lambda opened his mouth to reply, but instead bit his lip. Without a word, he stomped out of the tent.

Annika's weeping gradually subsided, slowly trickling out of her like a squeezed and empty juice box. She knew fierce bandits didn't cry, or at least seldom did; even the strongest bandit often cried before being hanged. *No crying unless you are about to be hanged.* That was written into the Code of the Bandit. Annika knew because she had read the entire code, all eight hundred pages of it, twice.

She had no proper schooling, but Annika had taught herself how to read, just as she had taught herself how to pick locks and perform basic feats of banditry. She had been proud to win the lock-picking contest, but had not dared to reveal the rest of her self-taught skills. She feared her father would not react kindly if he discovered she had been training herself in secret.

Her canvas tent door flapped open. Felipe wandered in, concern written on his face.

"Why is the word *concern* written on your face?" Annika asked.

Felipe rubbed the marker off his cheek. "Your weeping is bothering the weeping willows again."

"I don't care about trees!" shouted Annika. "Papa doesn't let me do anything." She scowled. "Papa." She repeated the word. It sat heavily on her tongue. "He's not even that."

"Curb your tongue," said Felipe. The squat bandit sat on the bed next to Annika. "He loves you, in his own way."

Annika didn't allow herself to take comfort in those words. She folded her arms. "He thinks all I'm good for is doing chores, like *fetch the ransom money* or *sharpen the knives so we can slice someone's neck*. He never lets me have fun."

Vigi Lambda's right-hand man patted Annika's hand, her right one, with his left. "It's hard for him. He could have killed you as a baby, you know. But he didn't, and there is nothing in the bandit code about raising a daughter. At least I don't think so. It's long and boring, so I've never actually read it." He mumbled the last part, blushing while staring at his shoes.

"I've read the entire thing. Twice," Annika exclaimed, swiping her hand away from Felipe's patting. "But not everything comes from a book, you know." She clenched her hands into fists and slammed them on the bedspread. "I'll show him. I'll prove I can be a great bandit, with or without him. I'll just have to . . ." Her voice trailed off with those last words, her mouth twisting into a frustrated grimace.

"What do you plan to do?" Felipe asked, worry rising in his voice. "Don't do anything rash, Annika."

"I'll do nothing," said Annika, lying down on the bed and rolling over, turning her back to Felipe. "What can I do? I'm just a worthless bandit girl who plays with rattles." She lifted the toy her father had given her earlier and shook it. "See?"

She continued to shake her rattle until Felipe left. As soon as her door flapped closed, Annika sat up straight. She had no intention of playing with baby toys or staying in the camp.

As soon as dinner was announced that night, the men would gather to eat. That would be her chance. The men would be too busy dining on burnt chipmunk, or charcoaled mongoose, or blackened geckos, or whatever animal the bandits had caught that day for dinner and then over-cooked, to notice Annika sneaking away.

Once free, she would prove she could rob and kidnap as ruthlessly as anyone.

She would need money for her journey. Before she left the forest, she would find a carriage to rob—any carriage would do, although a fancy one would be nice. Then, she would go far away, where she would rob and kidnap and prove she was the greatest bandit in the world. Then when she returned, her father, or more accurately the man who kidnapped her as an infant, would regret treating her like a child.

Annika spent the rest of the day practicing her knife throwing. She threw them into her pillow to muffle the sound. She always did that, which was why her pillow was now just a sheet with knife holes all over it, and wasn't very comfortable to sleep on. Fortunately for Annika, the men were too busy practicing their own knife throwing to notice the faint *thwick, thwick* coming from her tent.

Annika removed a small lock from under her pillow and a couple of bobby pins from her blonde hair. She often kept her hair up in bobby pins—they came in handy for lock picking. It was how she had won the bandit lock-picking contest.

She picked the lock, over and over again, while waiting for night to fall.

Finally, after what seemed like hours because it was

hours, Annika heard the dinner bell ring and the men gathering around the campfire to eat flaming snake tongue—it was hard to mistake its pungent odor. This was her chance. Clad in her bandit clothes—tattered and old and black-and-white to resemble a penguin—Annika grabbed a small bag she had packed and ducked out of her tent.

She stayed close to the trees, running noiselessly as bandits are taught to do. After twenty minutes of dashing and scurrying, she slowed. But it took longer than that, with the sun gone and the moon aglow, for her heart to ease its own racing.

The forest crickets creaked. The forest crows crowed. The forest bloodsucking iguanas sucked. Annika waited near the main road, the one that sliced through the forest, listening to the sounds, hoping to hear a carriage approach. She stood still, her knife gripped in her white-knuckled hand.

No carriage neared, and the longer Annika listened, the more depressed she felt. She couldn't run away without money and she couldn't go back to the bandit camp until she was ready to show everyone she was a fearsome bandit.

It was a shame that so few people drove carriages late at night anymore. After someone got robbed or kidnapped a few times, they tended to avoid riding a carriage through the forest, especially late at night.

After standing along the main road for so long her legs not only fell asleep but were snoring, Annika heard something coming toward her. Unfortunately, it was not the sounds of horses and rolling wheels. No, it was much more horrifying: the sound of rampaging and barking penguins.

Annika sprang up into the nearest tree and soon lay hidden amid its icy branches, peering down at the horde of penguins rushing along looking for trouble.

A creature ran with them, something that was penguin-like, but not entirely. It had the face and body of a penguin, but was taller and seemed more powerful. Large bushy eyebrows sat over glowing red eyes; horns sprung from its head and twin fangs hung from its beak. Still, its face looked familiar.

It was the boy from the carriage, the Baron's boy, but now a penguin beast. Annika was certain of that. She opened her mouth to call out to him, but then clamped her jaw shut.

He was one of them: a vicious, marauding, beastly bird. He was not human, or at least not mostly.

Annika quivered on her branch. She was not scared of much, but this sight frightened her.

When the penguins finally left, Annika fell into a well-earned sleep right there in the tree, her arms wrapped around a branch.

In the morning, the sun, its glow pale through the

branches, woke her. She yawned and jumped down to the ground.

She had only just landed when a hand grabbed her shoulder. The hand was bony yet strong, squeezing her with a deep, painful grip.

"This one will do," said an old woman in a gray and floppy witch hat, cackling. Annika recognized her as Blazenda, the Fortune Teller of Volgelplatz.

Annika spun and dug her hand into a leather pouch attached to her belt. She pulled out the weapon hidden in the bag, ready to fight.

She held a rattle.

"I must have grabbed this by mistake," she moaned.

Blazenda gripped one of Annika's arms, and someone else pinned her other arm behind her back. Other villagers emerged from the forest, one holding chains and another a large net.

Annika had nowhere to run.

24.
A Chant and a Chance

Alone in his room atop the ancient manor, Bolt slipped on a pair of clean tuxedo pants. The fresh, cottony smell of the clothes brought little comfort. He was still a prisoner in this tower and doomed for eternity, even if he was a remarkably well-dressed doomed prisoner.

A sound at the door interrupted Bolt's doom-filled thoughts. The knob turned and Frau Farfenugen entered. She held a platter of dead fish. They looked delicious, but Bolt pushed his appetite away. The housekeeper stared at Bolt. "Your pale face. Your hornlike hair. It has come to be. But then again, I'm just a lowly housekeeper, so what do I know?"

"Then it's true? I've turned into . . . I've become like the Baron?"

Frau Farfenugen shrugged.

"Tell me!" Bolt needed to hear the words. He grasped on to a last crumb of hope that maybe his nightmares had been merely dreams, as unlikely as it seemed.

"So, now you want to listen to me? I wasn't good enough to listen to the other night, was I, when I told you to stay in your room no matter what? But you turn into a penguin and I'm suddenly Miss Information." She spat and growled. "Don't you know? How can you not? At night the moon will turn you into a savage were-penguin. It is your curse. In many ways, worse than a werewolf!"

"Name one way."

"Well, maybe not worse. Equally horrible, I suppose. A were-anything is bad news across the board."

Bolt's stomach sank. "I need to get out of here."

"Leave? You cannot. The Baron will never let you go."

"But I must. The Baron's a madman. Or a mad boy. Or a mad penguin. He's mad, that's the point. The only thing I know for sure is that I need to leave." He would break the curse. If not, he would go far, far away, as far away from the Baron as possible.

"Even if you were freed from these walls, you would never escape," rasped Frau Farfenugen. "The Baron will hunt you down and then chew you up like gum and blow you into a giant bubble. Or worse. Do you want to be bubbled? Of course you don't. I have been trapped here for my entire life and now you will share my fate."

Bolt gasped but also scratched his head. "That's impossible. The Baron is just a boy. How could he have kept you here your whole life?"

"A boy? Don't make me laugh!" The housekeeper laughed. It was really just a wheeze, although Bolt assumed it was supposed to be a laugh. "The Baron is over one hundred years old."

"I don't believe it."

"Why should you? The Baron transforms into a penguin every night. That makes perfect sense. But living for more than one hundred years? Sure, I just made that up."

"OK, I guess I believe it," admitted Bolt.

The housekeeper looked away, and then back at Bolt, and then away again. "They say the Brugarian moon makes him immortal. It is bigger here. More powerful and always full. You will be just like him, soon, sharing his unquenchable thirst for raw fish and power. But it could be worse for you. At least you get the nice bedroom, while I have to sleep in the kitchen. Then again, I'm just a lowly housekeeper."

"Do you have to keep calling yourself a lowly housekeeper?"

"I could call myself a contemptible housekeeper, an undeserving housekeeper, or a loathsome housekeeper."

"No, let's keep lowly."

Frau Farfenugen sighed. "Very well."

"But there's a way to break the curse, right?" asked Bolt, biting his fingernails.

"Probably not. But *probably* is not *absolutely.*" Frau Farfenugen closed her eyes and chanted,

> *"When the moon is high, beware the mark,*
> *Where danger lurks and penguins bark.*
> *For you shall change, you shall transform,*
> *When penguin spirit inside is born."*

"I've heard that before," said Bolt.

"It hit number one in the Brugarian pop charts a few years ago. It's got a good beat and you can dance to it. But the second verse is less popular:

> *"Three days, that is all you have until*
> *The penguin curse inside you will*
> *Never stop nor never decrease,*
> *Until your humanity's deceased."*

"But it's just a song," said Bolt.

Frau Farfenugen frowned. She leaned over and whispered to Bolt, "It's just a song in the same way cupcakes are just a bread. Don't you understand? Three days. You only have three days to overcome the curse. Three days or you will never be human again. You spent one day in bed, sleeping, so you only have two days left."

"The Fortune Teller, Blazenda. She can help me, right?" asked Bolt quietly.

"She is your only chance," the housekeeper whispered back.

"I knew it!"

"Ssshh!" spat Frau Farfenugen, putting a finger to her lips. "We're whispering."

"Sorry. Right. Why are we whispering?" Bolt whispered.

"Because it makes our conversation feel extra creepy and suspenseful."

Bolt grabbed the housekeeper's arm. "Will you help me escape?" he asked in a semi-whisper.

"Me?" Frau Farfenugen shrieked, but quietly. "I cannot risk it. Not now. Not when I'm so close."

"Close to what?"

"Nothing," she said. "Forget I mentioned it." She yanked her arm from Bolt's grasp. As she did, a piece of paper fell from her apron. She picked it up and stuffed it back into her apron pocket, but not before Bolt noticed writing and hand-drawn hearts on it.

"What's that?" asked Bolt.

"What's what?"

"You were holding a note. With hearts."

"A note? I'm just a lowly housekeeper; why would someone give me a love letter?"

"A love letter? I just said it was a note."

"Exactly. No one would give me a love letter or a note."

Bolt shook his head. He would never get a love letter. Not that he wanted one, but the thought of never getting one, ever, was a little depressing. Penguin monsters didn't get love letters, just like Bolt would never have a family. Tears flowed down Bolt's face like water from a broken faucet.

The housekeeper stared at him. She sighed. "Stop that. I hate it when people get all sad and depressed about things. You need to be more optimistic, like me." She leaned closer to Bolt, and her whisper became extra whispery. "I will help you. Don't think this means we are friends. But if there's hope for you, maybe there's hope for me, too—hope for all of Brugaria. Legend has foretold a chosen one."

"That's what Blazenda told me. But chosen for what? I'm not brave or mighty."

"How do I know what you're chosen for? I'm just a lowly housekeeper. You could be chosen to fight the Baron. Or join him. Or do his laundry. I'm hardly an authority on these sorts of things." Frau Farfenugen still held the tray of dead fish. Now she turned it upside down and dropped the food onto the floor. Bolt's stomach growled as he watched. "The Baron cannot know I helped you or he might turn me into gum, or worse. Knock me out with this platter, and then you can escape down the staircase. The Baron is not home. It's your best chance."

She handed the platter to Bolt. He frowned. "Won't it hurt? I really don't want to hit you."

"Do it!" she commanded.

Bolt sighed, lifted the platter, and crashed it onto the housekeeper's head.

THUMP!

The housekeeper winced and then frowned. "All you've given me is a lump on my head. Harder, fool!"

"I'd rather not," admitted Bolt.

"Hit me!" she commanded.

Bolt hit her on her head again, harder.

THUMP!

Again, she winced. "Now I'll have two bumps."

"Sorry. I've never tried to knock anyone out before. Can't we just pretend I knocked you out?"

The housekeeper sighed and collapsed to the ground, amid the dead fish. As Bolt looked at her, she rasped. "Oh, look at me. I'm unconscious on the floor. I hope the prisoner doesn't escape." Bolt did not move. He looked down, feeling bad about the two lumps forming on the top of the housekeeper's head. Frau Farfenugen shook her head and growled. "Stop standing there staring. Run! Go into town and find the Fortune Teller before the Baron finds you. Break the curse. Or heaven help us all." She laid two cold fish atop her head. "And heaven help my head bumps."

25.

Escape from Chordata Manor

Dressed in his tuxedo, and with his black leather wingtip shoes laced tightly on his feet, Bolt darted across the lawn and toward the woods. The shoes were slippery on the snow-dusted grass. He almost fell, twice.

Bolt ran into the forest and thought he saw a penguin. His heart jumped.

But it was just a shadow.

Bolt plunged farther into the woods and its concealing darkness. Despite the dim light, he kept running, fearing birds or other menaces might be chasing him.

He saw a jackal about to leap out. No, it was a branch. He saw a cow monster ready to jump down. No, it was a nest.

He stopped for a moment, his neck throbbing and his legs too weak to run. When the transformation was complete, Bolt would be stronger. Mightier. Penguin-er.

The thought made him feel sick. He ran faster.

Bolt heard noises in the woods up ahead and froze. Perhaps the Baron had followed him. Or maybe a band of penguins was hunting for Bolt. He stood, too afraid to even breathe. But when he stopped, so did the noises.

Just my imagination, thought Bolt. *The woods are perfectly safe.*

Bolt ran past a giant pit filled with large animal bones. He jumped over a chasm filled with razor-sharp spikes. He slipped past a sign that read *Warning: giant snakes ahead.*

Perfectly safe, he repeated to himself.

Bolt constantly turned his head to see if anything followed. Nothing did, but by constantly turning his head, he almost smashed into fourteen different trees.

Soon, he heard more noises up ahead. These were not the barking of violent birds or the howls of crazed banshees—but the sounds of people. Happy shouts. Singing. He must be near downtown Volgelplatz. Bolt's heart leapt with joy. Bolt leapt for joy, too, although since he was still in the woods, he hit his head on a branch. He would need to remember not to leap again until safely away from trees.

He peeked out onto the main road. It was filled with people. Mothers and fathers danced with their children.

Teenagers ran hand in hand. Little kids skipped. Three people did cartwheels.

Bolt stepped out of the forest, but then hopped back in. These weren't people in the road—they were half-human and half-penguin mutants. What new horror was this? They were humanoid in form, but they had beaks and feathers. Some of these giant penguins wore shoes and lederhosen. There were tall ones and short ones, fat ones and thin ones. Had the Baron created these monstrosities in some sort of secret monstrosity lab?

Bolt was about to turn and flee back into the woods when he heard a child laugh, an innocent giggle. Nothing evil could giggle like that. He craned his neck past the tree he hid behind for a closer look.

A very tall penguin walked past him, so close Bolt could practically touch it. The creature held a giant banner in the air:

The Day of the Penguin

Of course! These weren't penguins, but people in fake beaks and penguin costumes. They were just normal, joyful Volgelplatzians (Volgelplatzers?) heading to the festival. It must be today.

Now Bolt could admire the penguin outfits without quaking. Unlike the tattered and meager costumes of the Brugarian Forest Bandits, these were carefully made, a kaleidoscope of bright and surprising colors. Some were furry and others were rubbery. One penguin costume was made out of seashells. A woman wore a costume built from what appeared to be orange seat cushions; she looked less like a penguin than a walking sofa.

The houses alongside the road were small and rustic, as cozy and quaint as Chordata Manor was imposing and cold. Many featured penguin flags waving from their roofs. The penguins depicted were proud and heroic birds with their chins and beaks held high, but they also appeared to be kind. None had horns or bushy eyebrows.

Many houses also had catapults on their roofs, although none as large as the Baron's contraption.

"Hey. You. Kid!" A finger tapped Bolt on the shoulder. Bolt turned and, when he saw the towering penguin next to him, screamed.

"Sorry. Didn't mean to scare you," said the man. He removed the fake penguin head he wore. "Going to the festival?" Bolt nodded. "I love your tuxedo. It's very penguin-like. But I thought you'd want one of these, too." The man handed Bolt a paper beak with a string around it. "Happy Penguin Day!" The man jogged off to join a woman and two young kids up ahead, all wearing fuzzy penguin suits. Bolt put on his beak. For one shining moment, he felt like he belonged here, just another penguin-costumed villager heading to the festival. Wasn't a village just a large family?

But the moment quickly dimmed. He wasn't here to *be-long*. He wasn't even here to help anyone. He was here to save himself. To break the curse. So his family, the family he would someday find, would accept him.

Bolt adjusted the beak and continued following the crowds into town. Everyone around him sang and laughed, pranced and danced, frolicked and scampered.

But not Bolt. He was the only one without a smile on his lips, the only person muttering to himself with furrows of determination upon his brow.

26.
The Day of the Penguin

As he entered the village, Bolt stared, wide-eyed. It was jam-packed. Everyone in town must have been there, and plenty more people, too. Bolt had never seen a celebration like this. Then again, the only parties he had ever attended were Mr. Smoof's yearly birthday bashes, in which the boys had to watch Mr. Smoof eat cake (he never shared) and open his presents. Each unwanted orphan also had to write an original haiku, such as:

Mr. Smoof's birthday
scarf is nice. May I wear it?
The heater's broken.

The town looked like an old German village, or at

least what Bolt imagined one looked like. Half-timbered buildings lined the narrow streets, with white plaster panels between dark wooden frames. An imposing church steeple, with stone walls and a tall rising spire, stood at the end of the block. Boisterous singing streamed from the many taverns and cafés.

An open-air market crowded the road, filled with dozens of makeshift shops selling penguin key chains, penguin snow globes, penguin pens, delicate glass penguin figurines, and other penguin-related souvenirs and treats.

And everywhere, people were dressed as penguins!

Villagers smiled and laughed. On one corner, four tuba players tooted a melody while four women in flowing red aprons tossed a pineapple back and forth. Two men clapped and sang, "Let's do the Penguin Pineapple Polka!" Little kids dressed like penguin chicks flitted about, playing tag and ducking in and around the grown-ups.

As he walked, amazed at the energy and antics all around him, Bolt passed a group of four girls jumping rope. He thought it must have been difficult to jump wearing rubber penguin feet, but the girls did, and jumped well. While they played, they chanted a rhyme. Bolt fought the urge to scream and run when he heard their song.

He was reminded that even here, among the joy, danger lurked.

"When the moon is high, beware the mark,
Where danger lurks and penguins bark.
For you shall change, you shall transform,
When penguin spirit inside is born."

They repeated the verse again, as if chanting a nursery rhyme. Bolt hurried past, cupping his hands over his ears and only lowering them once he was away from their song.

Bolt wandered deeper into the throngs and passed a group of fishermen. Bolt knew they were fishermen because they held nets and wore shirts that read *We Are Fishermen.*

"A killer whale was spotted off the coast," said one of the fishermen. "Everyone knows killer whales are enemies of penguins."

"I heard the same," said another. "Not a good sign during the festival."

"Plenty of bad signs recently," said the first man. "Our beloved penguins are growing meaner. Penguins attacked Helga and Burt last night. The teenagers will recover, but Burt lost a brand-new shoe . . ."

"Rubbish. They are just a few troublemaking penguins," responded a third fisherman. "I can't believe it means . . ."

Bolt didn't hear the rest of their conversation as the crowd pushed him forward. But their voices lingered. He remembered the night before. His memories. His dreams.

A large, tarantula-size ball of shame crept into his stomach.

As Bolt was propelled onward, he searched among the crowd. If the Fortune Teller was here, he didn't know how he would find her. If the Old and Seedy Part of Town was close, he did not know where to look.

Suddenly, Bolt stopped walking. His spine felt like it had been dipped in ice water. His mind sensed something—a roaring wind of anger and hate. He looked across the square in horror. The Baron! Although he was far away, it was as if the Baron's brain and Bolt's brain were wrapped together with string.

The Baron wore a paper penguin beak just like Bolt did, but there was no mistaking the hornlike hair or black penguin feather–sewn cape. It was he.

The Baron's mind was dark, as gray as the walls in Bolt's tower room. Such a craving for power! Such a deep, never-ending lust to rule!

The Baron turned and looked back. Had he sensed Bolt, just as Bolt had sensed the Baron? Bolt needed to run, to get out of sight. Anywhere. He squeezed through the crowd and ran to the first shelter he saw: the tall and imposing church now standing before him.

Bolt stepped inside and closed the thick wooden door, hoping this would be a haven where he could hide until it was safe. As he entered, he heard murmurs.

He was not alone.

27.

The Prince of Whales

Bolt stood in a small lobby with nothing but drab wooden walls and a cactus in a pot. Meanwhile, a church service appeared to be in session. Bolt peeked around the corner into the sanctuary.

About two dozen people sat in pews, heads bowed as if in prayer. Each congregant was dressed in a blue hooded fuzzy robe with a picture of a purple whale on the back. Each whale was happily swimming, giggling as if at a whale joke. In front, on the platform and behind a pulpit, stood a thin man, his back to the congregation. He wore the same uniform as the congregants, except his whale looked angrier, its mouth open to reveal sharp teeth, roaring and leaping from the sea.

A stained-glass window above the sanctuary depicted the same menacing whale.

Bolt slipped off his penguin beak and sat down in the back row, at the end, hidden by the shadows. He would stay until he was certain the Baron was no longer near. Fortunately, none of the others in the room paid attention to him.

The leader on the platform looked at the stained-glass window above. "O whale, thou mighty mammal." He waved a wooden club in the air. "Thou who art so very, very large, with such big teeth and an impressive blowhole."

"Blubber, blubber, blubber," chanted the audience.

"O hippo of the sea," continued the congregation leader, "splash us with thy fins. Sing to us thy songs. Fill us with thy spout-shooting water."

"Blubber, blubber, blubber," sang the audience.

The man on the platform turned and bowed. "Thank you for coming today." His voice—raspy and hoarse—echoed through the barren room.

Where had Bolt heard that voice before? It sounded familiar.

"As you know, this is the Day of the Penguin," said the speaker. "It is a day of celebration, but also a day of dread. For today we are reminded of our great victory, but also of the threats that still exist. For we are the sworn protectors of all of Brugaria. We are the Mystical Brotherhood of Whales."

The room became silent, until a woman sitting directly in front of Bolt cleared her throat. "Why do we call it the Mystical *Brotherhood* of Whales when the group includes men and women?" she asked "It's sexist, if you ask me. How about we call it the 'Mystical *Sisterhood* of Whales'?"

"Or the 'Mystical People-hood of Whales'?" asked another robed woman.

"Neighborhood of Whales?" suggested one of the male congregants. "That's sort of inclusive."

Others piped in. "Childhood of Whales . . . Robin Hood of Whales . . . Little Red Riding Hood of Whales? No, that doesn't work . . ."

"Enough!" the leader shouted. "It matters not what we are called. What's important is that the penguins are no longer acting like the joyful, happy creatures everyone loves. Must I remind you, it was the Brotherhood that fought the Great Bird Battle all those years ago? We built the catapults. We led the resistance. We have bided our time all these years, but now we must fight again!"

"Blubber, blubber," said one large man in the audience, but no one else joined in his blubbering.

"Why now?" asked the woman sitting in front of Bolt. "I'm supposed to go on vacation next week." Bolt ducked down, to avoid being seen.

"Then cancel your plans! Have you not seen the

signs?" The speaker thrust his wooden club in the air. No, it wasn't a club. It was a loaf of bread—a loaf of crusty French bread.

The man's hood inched off his head. It was the elderly Günter, whom Bolt had met in the Dead Penguin Inn.

"You are wrong!" shouted one of the robed men.

"The penguins are our friends!" shouted another.

"I really want to go on vacation and I've already paid for a hotel room," protested the woman in front of Bolt. Bolt squirmed and shrank lower in the pew, thankful the room was dimly lit.

"Blubber!" said the man who had blubbered alone a moment before. He stood up and pointed a finger at their leader. He was twice as wide as anyone else in the room. He had only two teeth.

"Yes, Franz?" asked Günter, lowering his loaf of bread.

"I know that you are the anointed prince of our Brotherhood. Or Sisterhood. Or whatever. But we have lived in peace with the penguins for years."

"So we have," agreed Günter. "But let us not forget the dark days when the Stranger came, one hundred years ago. No one cared that he waddled or walked around with a penguin egg. No one suspected he was secretly twisting the minds of the penguins and readying them for war. People ignored the signs. They dismissed the ransacking of fish shacks and the penguin tracks found in butter."

"That's how you can tell if a penguin is in your refrigerator," said someone in the audience. Others nodded their heads.

"The Stranger declared penguins were meant to rule. He demanded the people sit on penguin eggs until they hatched. He commanded our ancestors to bake fish sticks for them. He insisted we dress only in tuxedos."

Bolt looked at his tuxedo, and shrank farther into his seat.

"I know the tale," Franz said.

"Do you?" shouted their leader with a sudden French-bread jab. "Then you know of the storm, a winter squall unlike any the town had seen. You know of the endless lightning that crackled, and the dense, hazardous snow-flakes as big as onions."

"Red onions or yellow onions?" asked someone in the audience.

"Vidalia onions!" shouted Günter. The crowd gasped. "The clouds turned purple, and thunder cried out in fury. Thunder snow, they called it. Everyone agreed they had never seen a storm so fearsome."

"Blubber, blubber, blubber," chanted a few in the audience.

Bolt looked around the room, still thankful no one paid any attention to him.

As he spoke, Günter's voice grew louder and more forceful. "Then, as if the thunder trumpeted the start of war, the penguins came. The Stranger led them, crying, 'Penguins were meant to rule!' and 'Beware the penguins!' and 'Has anyone seen my keys?' because he had misplaced them. His army wrecked homes and looted fisheries. They didn't return library books they checked out. They tore tags from mattresses. But the Brotherhood refused to bow to the penguins. We led the fight."

"We led the fight," echoed a few voices in the crowd.

"Blubber, blubber, blubber," chanted others.

"The storm lasted for days," continued the prince. "Feet of snow piled high on the ground, and an endless volley of lightning lit the sky like flames. The penguins came every night, destroying then romping. And sometimes romping then destroying. Or even worse, both at the same time." He shivered.

"But the Brotherhood refused to surrender. We rained boulders from our rooftop catapults onto the evil

creatures. Many birds were beaten back, but still more came. Boulders flew through the nighttime sky, and the penguins barked and fought."

"Blubber, blubber, blubber," said a couple of people in the crowd.

"Blubber, blubber," echoed Bolt, carried away by the group's enthusiasm.

"Finally, the Brotherhood drove the Stranger away. They thought the Baron, the Stranger's evil assistant, was dead—although apparently they were misinformed. But since then we have lived in peace. Until now. The penguins grow bolder. Hordes of cruel penguins roam the countryside. Evil has risen again! Baron Chordata prepares for war!"

Upon the mention of his name, two men in the room screamed and fainted.

"Sorry," mumbled Günter.

"Yes, we know the Baron is evil and disturbing," said the woman in front of Bolt. "But . . ."

"And rotten," added another congregant.

"And rotten," agreed the woman.

"And deranged," said another person. "Don't forget deranged."

"OK. He's evil, disturbing, rotten, and deranged," agreed the woman. "Anything else?"

"Stinky?" suggested a man.

"Petulant?" said someone else.

Others piped in:

"Vile . . . Contemptible . . . Loathsome . . . Impolite . . . Vicious . . . Fun-loving, um, never mind that one . . . Menacing . . ."

"Fine! Enough!" cried the woman in front of Bolt. "Yes, the Baron—I won't speak his name to avoid any screaming and fainting—is all those things. But would he lead the penguins and start a war? Ridiculous. I don't believe it. I'm going on vacation."

The woman marched toward the main door. As all eyes watched her, Bolt sank farther in his pew.

"Come back!" cried Günter. He held up his French bread. "We must fight!"

The others stood and filed out, too. "You are wrong," they proclaimed. "We are at peace . . . I have nonrefundable hotel reservations . . ."

As the congregants left, Günter shouted to them, "Come back! Join me! Blubber, blubber, blubber!"

But they did not blubber back. Soon only Bolt, Franz, and Günter were left. Bolt was thankful for the shadows in the dim room, which continued to conceal him.

"Do you believe me, Franz?" Günter asked. "Something has changed, I tell you. Something bad, and the Baron is behind it. We need to arm the catapults. Or do you want to be attacked next?"

"I run the bowling alley," said Franz. "Penguins don't bowl."

"Not yet," warned Günter. "Do you want to take the chance they never will?"

"Bowling penguins," muttered Franz with a shiver. "Yes, that would be awful. The shoes wouldn't fit their webbed feet. Fine. I am ready to fight."

Günter clasped the larger man on his shoulder. At the same moment, his eyes shot across the room and rested on Bolt's pew-peeking head.

"You, there. Who are you?" He took a step forward, squinting. "Wait. Is that the Baron's boy?" Bolt stood up, staring at the loaf of French bread waving dangerously over Günter's head. "He's a spy! He hates whales!"

"I don't hate whales," said Bolt, stepping back. "To be honest, I don't really have an opinion about whales, good or bad."

"Get him!" yelled Günter to Franz.

Both Franz and Günter rushed forward.

28.
Sack of Rice

Bolt took a step toward the aisle. Günter neared, as did Franz, one coming from Bolt's right, the other his left.

"The Baron will regret this," rasped the Prince of Whales. "You will regret it."

"Blubber, blubber, blubber," agreed Franz, his mouth stretched into a mad two-toothed grin. He looked like a hockey player who refused to wear a mouth guard.

Bolt held out his hands. "You have it all wrong. I'm the Baron's prisoner."

"I don't see shackles," said Günter. "Or handcuffs. Or even very tight rubber bands."

"I escaped," said Bolt.

"Well, you won't escape us so easily." To Franz he shouted, "Now!"

They both lunged, but Bolt had already turned and jumped. He leapt higher than he thought possible, easily clearing the pew. Günter and Franz crashed into each other, their heads colliding with a painful *BANG!*

"The whale hater is escaping," groaned Günter as he crumpled to the floor.

"I'm telling you, I really don't hate whales," yelled Bolt as he dashed outside and into the thick crowd filling the streets. He slipped his paper penguin beak back into place.

It was easy to get lost in such a throng. Being a kid, and short, helped. Bolt pushed his way deeper within the masses. He ping-ponged between bellies and rear ends. It was quite unpleasant to shimmy and squirm among so many people, but Bolt felt certain his pursuers were falling farther and farther behind.

TOOT!

Bolt's head rang with the sound of a giant horn filling the streets. At first, Bolt thought the horn was for him, perhaps the Brotherhood sounding an ancient alarm. But the crowd surged toward the center of town, paying no attention to Bolt. The horn blared again, and the people swept forward even faster. Bolt was carried along with the rabble. He couldn't have fought against the crowd even if he tried.

Fortunately Bolt did not see the Baron, or feel his presence. Nor did he see anyone from the Brotherhood, or Sisterhood, or whatever it was called. For now, he felt safe. But he had not forgotten his curse, and his need to find the Fortune Teller.

The hordes, carrying Bolt along, turned the corner and poured into a large town square—an enormous open space with a tall wooden stage erected in the center. On the stage sat an elaborately carved silver throne with plush red velvet upholstery. Next to that stood a scaffold with a noose.

A noose for hanging.

Bolt wiggled closer to the stage until he was right in front of it. The noose must be a prop—it wasn't meant for an actual hanging. Nothing so horrible could be part of such a joyous celebration.

Somewhere a bugle blasted, loud and long, and all eyes turned to the far side of the square. A group of people, both men and women, emerged from a cobblestone path that curved between the buildings, all dressed in large matching penguin costumes. Some of the people danced and others played horns or drums. The group of penguin musicians and dancers wiggled through the crowd like a serpent, its tail expanding as others joined the snakelike weaving. The line was soon fifty people long, then one hundred, then more.

The music was odd, if it could be called music—random beeps and burps, a menagerie of awfulness. Bolt covered his ears. It sounded like terrible musical barking.

Of course. The band's tune mimicked the barking of penguins. The sound became more and more captivating, and Bolt found himself barking along.

A woman in a floppy gray hat and a long black wedding dress with spiderweb-like lace led the procession. Even from far away Bolt knew it was Blazenda, the Fortune Teller. If only Bolt could talk to her! But there was no way to get her attention amid the crowd.

Blazenda and the penguin dancers spun and barked. With each stomp of the drum or toot of a horn, they yelled the same chant:

"Sack of rice!"

Everyone yelled the chant now, thousands of people. Even Bolt shouted, although he had no idea why a sack of rice was so important. The crowd's voice grew louder and louder, the drumming fiercer and fiercer, the horn playing barkier and barkier, and the group snaked closer and closer.

As they reached the stage, Blazenda ascended the steps. She was only a few feet away from Bolt, and he yelled her name and jumped up and down, but she did not see nor hear him among the crowd, which was filled with people also jumping and screaming. The dancers and musicians backed away, leaving only two short men dressed as penguins to follow Blazenda up the stairs. The other dancers and musicians blended in with the crowd.

The two men held a billowy purple cushion. A penguin sat atop it. The bird wore a golden crown dotted with jewels.

"Sack of rice!" screamed the crowd.

"Sack of rice!" echoed Bolt.

The penguin looked around from its perch, its eyes darting back and forth. As the men placed the penguin on the silver throne on the stage, Bolt could sense its nervousness. He could read the penguin's thoughts: *What's going on? I want to go home. Who has fish sticks?*

Bolt could feel the bird's breathing, hear its beak creaking, and detect its webbed feet shaking.

"All hail the Penguin King!" shouted Blazenda.

The throngs cheered, a deafening roar, and then someone from the crowd screamed, "Let loose the fish!"

"Let 'em fly!" screamed another.

Led by the Fortune Teller onstage, the crowd began counting down. "Ten, nine, eight, seven . . ."

The excitement was as thick as a walrus's belly.

"Three, two, one . . ."

A bugle blasted and a multitude of catapults, one on nearly every building, flung their arms up into the sky. Bolt cringed, expecting to be smashed by rocks or boulders, until he realized the catapults had heaved fish, millions of them flying in a majestic and beautiful arc. They clouded the sky with their gray bodies, and then fell and splattered everywhere: on the street, on benches, on other buildings, on the stage, and on people. Two flopped on Bolt's head, nearly dislodging his paper beak.

"We toss fish in memory of the great battle!" yelled Blazenda from atop the stage. The crowd erupted in applause and screams.

The smell of dead fish rose up from the ground. Fish bits stuck in Bolt's hair and he pulled the wet, slimy nuggets off and plopped them into his mouth.

His stomach yearned to eat more. He thought people might become suspicious if he started inhaling fish carcasses, so he fought the urge to get down on his knees and nosh.

The crowd was silent. No one moved. They were waiting for something.

Blazenda pointed to the middle of the crowd. The crowd turned, following her finger.

Three people approached the stage. The villagers stepped aside to give them room to pass. Bolt assumed two of the people were prison guards, because they wore dull gray uniforms and their caps read *We Are Prison Guards.* The third person was a girl in a tattered outfit that looked vaguely penguin-like. She trudged forward, one of the guards holding her arm to keep her from running. The guard led her up the steps and toward the scaffold and its noose.

Bolt blinked. Their prisoner was Annika, the girl bandit. Her long blonde hair flowed freely, no longer constrained by a penguin cap, although part of it appeared to be held up by a bobby pin.

As Bolt watched, a lump formed in his throat and his heart beat like a bongo drum. They were going to hang her? No, it must all be an act. Make-believe.

"Today is the Day of the Penguin!" Blazenda bellowed as the guards slipped the noose over Annika's neck. "Today we honor our penguin ancestors. As in the days of yore, the penguins demand a sacrifice."

"Sacrifice!" yelled the crowd, which Bolt realized was what they had been saying all along, and made a lot more sense than "sack of rice." He blushed a little.

Annika stood straight, staring ahead, defiant.

The Fortune Teller returned Annika's stony glare. "This girl is a criminal, one of the evil forest bandits. She is guilty of crimes against us. And crimes against us are crimes against the penguins."

The crowd roared. Annika glowered at the mob, and while her eyes did not tear up, the look of terror was impossible to miss. Those terror-filled but dry eyes rested on Bolt.

Sure, she had tried to kidnap him. Yes, she was a vicious bandit. Also, she had been rather unpleasant in the

forest the other night. But she was just a kid, like Bolt. Annika hadn't slit Bolt's throat, even after he had gulped loudly, and didn't one good turn deserve another? Bolt couldn't let her die.

"The penguins demand a sacrifice!" the Fortune Teller howled.

The crowd chanted, "Yes! Yes!"

"The penguins demand a life!"

"Penguins! Penguins!"

Blazenda put her arm on the lever to release the bottom of the scaffold. If Bolt didn't do something, the floor would open, Annika would fall, and the noose would snap her neck. The hairs on the back of Bolt's neck stood up. He looked at the Penguin King; he felt the feathers on the back of its neck standing up, too.

Bolt sensed the penguin's fear and its confusion.

And the bird sensed Bolt.

Bolt thought: *Save her! Obey me! I am one of you!* He hammered the Penguin King with his thoughts. Orders. They were connected, Bolt and the Penguin King. Linked. Two birds of a feather.

The Fortune Teller released the lever. The penguin jumped. The floorboards swung open.

Penguins are tremendous leapers. The Penguin King sailed forward and its beak pierced the rope before it grew taut. The rope snapped, and Annika fell to the ground below the platform, free from the noose.

Then the Penguin King jumped into the crowd, biting and yelping a violent bark.

"The king! He's gone mad!" yelled a man in the crowd, the penguin snapping at him, the people stampeding to escape, and Bolt watching in shock and horror.

29.
The Tunnels

top! Bolt's mind shouted to the Penguin King.
Bolt tried to force his voice into the bird's brain
as it ran around, snapping at terrified villagers.

But he couldn't get through to the bird.

Something was blocking Bolt.

But Bolt could hear thoughts hammering themselves
into the penguin's clouded mind—thoughts that came
from someone else.

Hurt people! Bite! No fish sticks for you!

The Baron. He stood on the opposite side of the platform, snarling and muttering to himself.

No, muttering to the Penguin King, ordering it to
attack.

At the same moment that Bolt stared at the Baron,

the Baron looked up and stared back at Bolt. Their eyes locked. Bolt could hear the Baron's voice echo inside him.

We were meant to rule! We are one! We are BFFs!

Bolt turned to run, to escape, clearing the Baron's mad thoughts from his head as best he could. But there were so many people running and panicking that it was hard to move anywhere. Bolt stumbled through the rioting, frightened mob. People shoved and scrambled in random directions. Bolt was knocked and bumped. He spun and reeled.

Bolt felt a warm hand grabbing his shoulder, halting his spinning and reeling. He flinched, expecting the worst.

It was Annika.

"Are you kidnapping me?" asked Bolt, as a man ran into them both, screamed, and then kept running. "Because I'm sort of busy trying not to get trampled."

"No, I'm not kidnapping you. Not now. But if you want to get out of here, follow me."

Annika was quick, ducking between the legs of a man wearing a cumbersome penguin costume and leaping around a woman on crutches. She sidestepped a man holding a heavy tuba and rolled past another man carrying a stack of bricks.

She seemed to find every small crevice between villagers, every hole that was wide enough to wiggle through or squeeze past. More than once she stopped to wait for

Bolt, who was slower and clumsier than she. His wingtip shoes didn't help his speed or nimbleness. The soles were still slippery.

Annika jumped around three men and then rolled around another. Bolt jumped and rolled, too, but he was stopped mid-somersault by someone's foot. A hand grabbed his arm and yanked him to his feet.

"I've got you now, whale hater!" yelled Günter. He still wore his fuzzy Brotherhood robe. "Franz! I have him!" The crowd rushed around them, but no one stopped. The mob was in an uncontrollable panic, too frenzied to pay them attention.

"Let me go! And I don't hate whales," yelped Bolt. He tried to tear his arm loose, but the man's grip was strong, and Bolt was not.

"He is in league with the devil!" yelled Günter, waving his bread. A few people turned to look at Bolt and screamed, but everyone was already screaming, so it was hard to say what exactly they were screaming about: Bolt, the French bread, or just from the general chaos.

Günter raised his loaf. It looked crustier and harder this close, so near Bolt's head. "I should have fed you to the alligators, if only we had some alligators. But you'll be sorry you dared mess with the Brotherhood."

"Or maybe the Sisterhood, or something else," said a passing stranger in the crowd.

Bolt again tried to free himself, but could not. Had

Bolt escaped the Baron's manor only to meet his end here, in a panicked crowd, beaten by overbaked bread?

Someone pushed Günter from behind. "Hey!" he cried, stumbling forward and releasing his grip on Bolt, his arms flailing.

The crowd swallowed him as Annika grabbed Bolt's hand. "Come on!"

As Günter shoved his way back through the crowd, Annika and Bolt dashed the opposite way, tumbling and ducking through the panicking villagers. "I'll get you, whale hater!" the prince cried, his voice already distant.

"The boy really doesn't look like he hates whales," said someone racing by them.

Soon the mob thinned, and Bolt and Annika sprinted out of the village square and down a narrow stone path that ran along the side of a small building. From the disrepair of the path, and the weeds sprouting up between the stones, it was clear this was not a path used often. The trail wound past the building's lawn and twisted into a clump of trees. Annika pointed at a circular reddish iron door in the ground covered by a thin layer of dirt. She knelt down, wiped away the dirt, and raised the cover, which lifted with a rusty squeak. "In here!"

"What's down there?" asked Bolt. Although he had often bolted under beds, he did not enjoy the thought of bolting underground.

Annika jabbed him. "Quick! Go!"

Bolt peered down into the dark, unlit hole. "Maybe we can hide somewhere sunnier?" Annika frowned, jabbed again, and Bolt sighed. He scampered down a small ladder leading into blackness. Annika followed, but not before pushing the cover back in place, smothering any light.

After only descending a few steps, the ladder ended. "Drop," Annika ordered.

"But I don't see anything."

"You'll be fine, I promise you. And bandits always keep their word, or at least usually. It's part of the Code of the Bandit, which I've read twice."

Bolt knew nothing of bandit codes but took a leap of faith, literally, and dropped down. After only a few feet, Bolt landed on soft, spongy dirt. He scampered out of the way so Annika could drop down without landing on top of him.

The place smelled of earthen clay and rot. It was quiet, the sounds from above completely silenced. Bolt stood, rigid, as a feeling of panic rose inside him. He wondered if these dark spaces were filled with moles and moths, like the dark spaces back at the orphanage.

He waited for a mole to bite his feet.

A light blazed to the side. Annika stood, holding a torch and blowing out a match. With the flame she lit a series of gas lamps that hung on the wall. Their flames crackled and lit the cavernous space in a fiery glow, casting moving, distorted shadows upon the walls. "We're fine. For now," said Annika.

"Where are we?" asked Bolt. His voice echoed. Three paths led from the recess where they stood, each plunging into darkness. Bolt felt like he was in another world, a dark and dirty world, but at least a world where he wouldn't be trampled by frenzied mobs.

"These tunnels were built during the Great Bird Battle," explained Annika. The lantern flames flickered against her deep-green eyes. "They come in handy for making quick bandit getaways."

"So you come down here a lot?"

"No, my papa says I'm too young to rob and kidnap— and he's so wrong about that, by the way—but I've studied the maps. There are many secret tunnels throughout the village and in lots of buildings and houses, if you know where to look for them." Annika pointed to the three passageways. "I think that tunnel leads to the forest. I'm pretty sure that one leads out of Brugaria. And that one must lead to the Fish Stick Stand—running around tunnels all day can make you hungry." She jabbed her finger toward the middle tunnel. "I'm taking that tunnel, the one out of Brugaria. There aren't enough carriages driving around here for me to kidnap someone, and I need to prove I'm the greatest bandit who ever lived."

Bolt stared at the tunnels. He stepped toward one,

shook his head and stopped, and stepped toward another, then shook his head and stopped and stepped toward another, and then repeated doing this over and over again, unsure which path to take.

"Stop doing that," said Annika. "It's annoying."

"But what should I do?" wailed Bolt. "Run? Eat fish sticks? Or just continue taking small steps toward various tunnel entrances?"

"One of the first two, please."

Bolt took a deep breath. If he went with Annika, maybe he could escape the Baron. He would turn into a penguin, of course, but there were worse things, maybe? He couldn't think of any, but maybe life wouldn't be so bad, as long as he was free of the Baron's diabolical clutches.

But his legs didn't move toward the middle tunnel. For the first time Bolt could remember, he was hesitant to bolt from real danger.

What sort of life would he live, if he bolted now? He would never have a family, not a real family, anyway. That was all he had ever wanted. Was he truly prepared to bolt from that? Wouldn't he risk everything for that chance, even if the chance was but a thin whisper of one?

He was so lost in thought and indecision and taking small steps toward the tunnels that he didn't notice Annika stepping toward him. "You look different, more penguin-like, and I saw you last night running with the penguins. I want to know what's going on."

Bolt shook his head. "I can't tell you. It's all too horrible."

"As we ran through the crowd I grabbed a book of matches, three used tissues"—she paused, scowled, and wiped her fingers on her pants—"and this." She removed a knife from her belt and inched it toward Bolt's neck, so the metal touched his skin. "Maybe I should slit your throat."

"I guess I can tell you," said Bolt, with a gulp. "And sorry about the loud gulping. I know you don't like that."

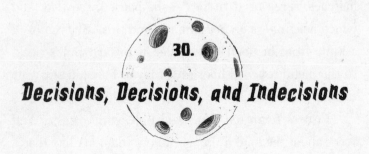

30.

Decisions, Decisions, and Indecisions

Annika leaned against the tunnel wall, the back of her tattered penguin clothing clinging to the moisture in the dirt, her knife held loosely in her hand. She straightened and brushed off some mud on her shoulder. She thought about everything Bolt had just told her.

As she had suspected, the penguins were growing bolder, nastier.

As she had feared, the Baron was planning on using them to start a war.

And as she had believed possible, even though it seemed impossible, Bolt was turning into a werepenguin. He could talk to the penguins, too. He had even saved Annika's life.

It was a lot to take in. Annika rubbed her finger on the

underside of her knife's blade. It calmed her. Unlike a were-penguin, a knife didn't turn into something else at night, such as a fork or a spoon. It just was. The knife didn't just make her feel grounded. It made her feel strong. Powerful.

She might not be the greatest bandit who ever lived, at least not yet. But she had escaped a frenzied mob. She had picked pockets and stolen a knife and matches. She hadn't even cried during the hanging even though many bandits cried before hanging, and it was explicitly allowed by the Code of the Bandit.

Let the penguins attack—she was armed and ready for them!

Or not.

Who was she kidding?

She stomped her foot. She couldn't even escape from a simple hanging by herself. She had to be saved by some skinny non-bandit boy. She was grateful—how could she not be?—but also embarrassed. The greatest bandit who ever lived would never need help from anyone, even if that someone could speak to penguins.

But even more than the frustration she felt from needing Bolt's assistance to escape the villagers, even more than the yearning that burned inside her head to prove her bandit mettle, one dreadful question plagued her:

What will happen to the Brugarian bandits if the Baron wages war?

No, when *he wages war?*

A moment ago, Annika had not doubted what she should do next. She would run away and practice banditry. Kidnapping! Robbery!

But now? How could she abandon her family *now*?

The bandits had a bargain with the Baron. He left them alone as long as they paid a kidnapping tax. Annika doubted the Baron would keep that truce.

She had to warn the bandits, but she also knew her father was stubborn. If she went home to warn them, would her father even believe her? He was as hard and untransformable as the knife in her hand.

A sound interrupted her thoughts. The cover above them slid open with a loud metallic scrape. Bolt stood, seemingly frozen, staring up as sunlight poured into the dim, hand-dug tunnel.

Annika ran down the nearest tunnel, then stopped, plastered herself against the wall, and let the darkness swallow her. She controlled her breathing, like an experienced bandit spy.

"There you are, Bolt," said the Baron, dropping down into the tunnel, landing on his feet and grinning. "I know about these tunnels, of course. I've studied them for many years." Bolt stood, his legs shaking, his knees clacking loudly against each other. "It's a shame you made the Penguin King snap that noose. A good hanging is hard to find these days. But still, it was impressive. You haven't even fully transformed into a werepenguin and you're already ordering birds around. You are a natural commander. We will make a fine team."

"I will never lead the penguins into war," said Bolt. Although his legs quaked, his voice was steady. It sounded almost firm and cruel. Annika watched, impressed.

"When your transformation is complete, I will make sure you want nothing else," said the Baron with a chuckle. "But now you're coming back with me."

Annika stepped forward.

She knew fighting the Baron alone wasn't the smartest idea. He was powerful and cunning, and she would never become the greatest bandit who ever lived by foolishly fighting enemies that were powerful and cunning.

But she owed Bolt for saving her life, and bandits always paid their debts. Even more than that, she needed him. Just one look at the were-monster that Bolt was becoming, one glimpse at his face, revealed the terrible truth of the war to come. With Bolt, maybe she could convince her father of the threat they were up against. Even a knife can bend with enough heat.

Better still, she could defeat the Baron right now. What better way to show her father how fierce a fighter she could be?

Annika inched out of the tunnel. "Hold it right there. Bolt isn't going anywhere with you."

The Baron turned, surprised. But when he saw Annika, he didn't shake. He didn't even seem worried. Instead, he laughed and then yawned. "And what do you think you can do?"

Annika held the knife in front of her. "Plenty. I'm the greatest bandit who ever lived."

She only wished those words were true.

31.

You Don't Want to See Me Very Angry

Although Bolt wanted to bolt as far away as possible, he somehow kept himself standing in place. But staying put was not the same as being brave and mighty enough to fight. So he stood rooted to the spot, watching Annika advance.

The tunnel lights glimmered on Annika's knife as she approached the Baron. The Baron smiled. "You're the bandit girl, aren't you? The one Bolt freed."

Annika stiffened. "I didn't need the help, you know." The Baron giggled and rolled his eyes. "Well, not mostly." The Baron giggled again, and Annika wiggled her knife. "Giggle all you want. I'm not afraid of you." The Baron arched his eyebrows and giggled even louder. "OK, maybe I'm a little afraid of you," Annika admitted.

"But I'm going to stop you anyway." She held her head up. "I am the greatest bandit who ever lived. Or I will be. Surrender, or fight!"

The Baron did not move. He did not run. He twisted the hair on his head, so that the hairs pointed up into taller hair horns. "Surrender or fight? How about if I pick a third option—let someone else do my bidding."

Bolt felt something slam against his head. No, it was inside his head. It felt like tentacles wrapping themselves around his brain, as if an octopus had crawled inside his ear.

We are BFFs!

The Baron whispered the words, but they felt like a siren screaming across Bolt's brain. His mind grew cloudy, and the words echoed as he stepped toward Annika, his arms outstretched to grab her.

Penguins are meant to rule! We must stop anyone in our way!

"What are you doing?" Annika shrieked, staring at Bolt while he grew nearer, his mouth open as if baring fangs, although he had no fangs to bare. She waved her knife toward him, and then toward the Baron and then toward Bolt, back and forth. "No one move."

Bolt gritted his teeth, pushing the evil Baron thoughts from his head. Back and forth, back and forth. It was like a terrible tug-of-war. Bolt's brain swarmed with urges to commit violence and then urges to push out the violence. He put his hands to his head and reeled back. Then he reeled forward toward Annika. And then he reeled back. And then he reeled forward toward Annika again.

"I'm getting dizzy," complained the Baron.

Bolt clenched his teeth and jammed the Baron's thoughts from his head, through his ear, and out into the dark tunnel. He stood, panting, sweat dripping from his head and onto his tuxedo jacket. His mind was clear.

"Impressive," said the Baron. "But your ability to fight against my control will not come as easily once the transformation is complete."

"I guess it's just you and me now," grunted Annika, her knife still held in her hand.

"Hardly," said the Baron with a yawn.

There was a low shuffling noise from above, metal against stone. The Penguin King, still wearing his golden crown, dropped down from the now-opened tunnel hole and landed next to Annika. The bird, its eyes staring blankly, swatted her hand with a wing. The knife thudded against the tunnel's earth floor.

Another swat from the penguin's wing collided against Annika's leg. She stumbled and twisted awkwardly. She fell and her head banged against the ground.

Annika lay still, unmoving.

Bolt hadn't moved since he had shot the Baron's orders out his ear. He stared at Annika, wondering if it would be possible to grab her and bolt. Or if he could somehow fight the Baron himself. Or if, better yet, he should continue standing where he was, too scared to do much of anything, and maybe the Baron would forget he was there.

Bolt's ear twisted painfully. The Baron held Bolt's lobe. "Did you think I'd forget about you? Let's go home, Bolt. Chordata Manor is your home, forever." To the Penguin King, he said, "Bring that girl. The dungeon hasn't had a prisoner in ages. The rats could use someone to nibble on."

Bolt lurched, his legs ready to bolt. Or fight. Or do nothing.

The Baron pinched Bolt's ear tighter. "Oh, I wouldn't try to do anything except obey me, or I'll be very angry," he said. "And you don't want to see me very angry." He twisted Bolt's ear even more, forcing him down one of the tunnels. "I will need to keep a closer eye on you, it seems. But we will be BFFs for eternity—whether you like it or not."

32.

The True Story of the Baron and the Great Bird Battle

Bolt stood next to his bed in the tower while the Baron blocked the doorway, arms crossed.

"Why so glum?" asked the Baron with a smug grin.

"Soon I'll be a power-hungry were-creature for eternity," Bolt moaned. "If you can't be glum about something like that, when can you be glum?"

"Did you ask a question?"

"Just a rhetorical one. It hardly counts."

The Baron raised his arms and pumped his fists "Oh, Bolt. You should be excited. You're a leader. An emperor. An emperor penguin, in a way."

"I'm cursed," Bolt groaned softly.

"No!" the Baron shouted, pounding his fist against the

palm of his other hand. "You are not cursed, but blessed! You are no longer one of *them*." He spat when he said *them* as if the word was distasteful. "One of the commoners, like that bandit girl wallowing in my dungeon below. Don't you see? You were once just an unwanted boy. But now you're a ruler."

"I don't want to rule."

"Tough noogies."

Bolt slumped.

The Baron stepped closer and clapped Bolt on the back. Bolt's entire body shivered with disgust at the Baron's touch, but the Baron didn't seem to notice. "As you grow into your powers, you will see the truth. Look!" The Baron tore open his tuxedo jacket, ripping off three buttons. Bolt stared in horror at the Baron's bare stomach.

Right over the Baron's belly button was a large penguin birthmark, identical to the one on Bolt's neck.

"Yes, I have it, too!" cried the Baron. "The mark! Don't you wonder why you can understand the penguins? Why you can talk to them? You think everyone has these talents? Oh, they are talents—the greatest of them all. The talents to be a penguin."

Bolt stared at the Baron's stomach. Then he glanced at his own mark, or at least tried to glance at it, but he couldn't because the mark was on his neck. As he stared at the Baron, and tried to stare, unsuccessfully, at his own mark, despair flooded into Bolt's head so fast, he felt as if it might pour out of his mouth. Instead, a piece of spittle flung from his lips as he spoke. "I d-don't want to be a p-penguin."

The Baron stepped slightly to the left to avoid the spit. "Too late now."

Bolt wrapped his arms around his body and rocked in place, filled with hopelessness. Quietly he groaned, "I just want my real family."

"*Real family?*" repeated the Baron, his voice booming. "Families are overrated. You think I need a family? Of course not. I haven't had a family for one hundred years, next Wednesday. I had one long ago. Once, I was like everyone else. Weak. Worthless. But then a Stranger came to town. He'd heard of my mark, you see—the mark we share, you and I. A mark of greatness! And because of it, the Stranger plucked me from my drab and lackluster life. Just like I plucked you from yours."

"You were rich and living in a manor," Bolt pointed out.

"Well, maybe my life wasn't all that drab. But still, he rescued me from a life of mediocrity. A werepenguin can't just bite anyone and turn them into an immortal penguin ruler, you know. Oh, if only we could! Can you imagine anything more wonderfully perfect than a world with thousands of werepenguins running around?"

"Actually, I can think of quite a few things more wonderfully perfect. Like, just about anything else."

The Baron ignored the comment. "All I needed to do was agree to be bitten, one simple bite on the neck, and I would become a werepenguin for eternity. I readily agreed to his bargain. A werepenguin is powerful, but two werepenguins, side by side? We would be unstoppable."

"So, that's why you bit me."

"I didn't bite you for the fun of it, although admittedly it is sort of fun biting people. But your neck was a little grimy. I had to brush my teeth twice afterward."

"Sorry. The bathtub pipes were broken at the orphanage."

"The sea will clean you so you'll never have to bathe again. That's one of the perks of being a werepenguin." He paused and scratched his chin. "Where was I in my story?"

"You agreed to the Stranger's bargain and were bitten."

"Ah, yes. Of course. My parents didn't understand. They wanted me to see a doctor. Or a vet. Or maybe even a marine biologist. As if they could cure me. As if I wanted to be cured! I ordered my parents to leave Brugaria or I would stuff them with treats and beat them like piñatas. They fled, which was a shame since I've always wanted to play with a piñata." He sighed. "Maybe someday." Bolt stepped back, recoiling from the Baron's words.

Bolt couldn't imagine ever turning away from his real

family. If he didn't stop his transformation, would he truly be like the Baron? Would he never want a family? The mere thought made Bolt shudder.

"But I don't understand something," said Bolt. "You said two werepenguins fighting side by side could never be stopped. But you *were* stopped. By the Brotherhood of Whales, or Sisterhood, or whatever they are calling themselves."

The Baron had been walking back and forth, preening like a peacock showing off its feathers. Upon hearing Bolt's question he stopped and let loose a loud, ferocious penguin bark that made Bolt jump back, his legs hitting his bed frame, and he fell on top of its covers.

"You refer to those whale lovers?" ranted the Baron. "They are fakes! Charlatans! Phonies! I know they take credit for winning the Great Bird Battle. They fought us with those silly catapults. But we were winning the war and had stockpiled a year's supply of fish sticks. Meanwhile, the Brotherhood had almost run out of boulders. I was certain victory would soon be ours! The Stranger was so convinced he even began a victory dance, and it's not easy to dance with webbed feet. He was quite impressive. Then a villager flung a slice of lasagna. Apparently it was dinnertime and someone made a mistake."

"I've never had lasagna," Bolt said to himself. The closest he'd come was spaghetti, although Bolt always suspected the yellow noodles served at the orphanage were actually old shoelaces. He doubted real spaghetti had aglets.

"The pasta dish missed us," continued the Baron, "but the Stranger was too busy dancing to notice. He stepped on the lasagna and banged his head. When he awoke, he had amnesia. His link to the penguins was broken. The birds lost their will to fight. I had only been a werepenguin for a few days, and did not yet know how to control them alone. As I was yelling at the birds to come back and fight, a catapult-launched boulder landed on me. It nearly killed me! If a band of loyal penguins hadn't dragged me back to the manor, who knows what might have happened? But eventually I healed. They say the Brugarian moon makes our kind immortal. They also say, 'Poor kid poured curd pulled cod,' although that is better left unsaid."

"I've heard that," agreed Bolt.

"Now I am stronger than ever, and my shoes are slip-resistant." He lifted one of his boots to show its rubber sole. "Lasagna doesn't frighten me."

"What happened to the Stranger?"

"During that final battle he wandered off, confused, looking for somewhere to lay an egg. I'm not sure what happened after that. I waited for him to return, hoping his head would clear and he would fight anew. But he never did. I have heard of a penguin colony at the South Pole that follow an odd, abnormally large penguin with thick eyebrows. But those may be only rumors. No matter. I don't need him. With your help, all of Brugaria will obey me."

"The people will fight you."

"Then they will lose." The Baron chuckled, although it soon turned into a boisterous laugh, and Bolt quivered. "After I recovered, I decided I needed an heir. I discovered a girl with a bird birthmark, but it was the shape of a flamingo. I heard of a boy and went to great lengths to bring him to me, but his birthmark turned out to be shaped like a goose. There were others, like a set of triplets with identical ostrich-shaped freckles on their feet. I had nearly given up hope of ever finding someone who could join me. But then I saw your picture in a small hospital newsletter from America—a funny infant born with a strange birthmark on his neck. There was no doubt you were the one."

"But if you found me as an infant, why did you wait—?"

"—twelve years to claim you?" Bolt nodded. "Do you think I wanted to? Of course not! Finally, I had found someone to fight with me! Or do my laundry! Or both!"

"I could fight against you," said Bolt.

The Baron waved his hand, as if the idea was worthless. He continued his story, only stopping to add some disturbing laughter. "I offered your parents riches if they gave you to me. They declined my offer." Disturbing laughter. "I offered them power—'Rule with me!' I cried—but they said, 'Thank you, but no thank you.' They were very polite." More disturbing laughter. "Finally, I demanded they hand you over, or I would get very angry, boil them into caramel, and pour them over ice cream, and maybe strawberries and other treats." Lots and lots of disturbing laughter.

"They wanted me?" asked Bolt, the words barely croaking from his throat. "They loved me?"

The Baron did not seem to hear Bolt, as he was still laughing in a disturbing way. "Your parents still refused. So I sent a dessert chef to their house to prepare the caramel sauce. Your parents fought, the caramel sauce caught fire, and the house was burnt to a crisp, as was everyone inside it. Or so I believed. I discovered years later that the chef fled with you in his arms, then dropped you at an orphanage in the middle of the night. Don't worry, the chef received his just desserts." More laughter, and this laughter was so disturbing, Bolt shrieked.

Bolt thought of the picture of the chef on the wall near the fireplace below, and shrieked even louder.

The Baron only smiled. "Meanwhile, I continued planning my rule, slowly warping the minds of all the Brugarian penguins. It took many years and lots of raw fish. But then, just when my schemes were complete and the penguins ready for battle, I stumbled across a news story about a moth infestation in the town of Oak Wilt. There you were, in a photo. While I couldn't make out your face, since it was covered by moths, your birthmark was as plain as day. I sent for you immediately. And now you're here! Isn't that joyful?"

Bolt was filled with conflicting emotions, but none of them was joy.

He would never meet his parents, because they were dead. The evil Baron was evil in all sorts of ways Bolt hadn't realized. And Bolt would soon be just like him.

All of Bolt's dreams spilled out of him like he was a ripped bag of groceries, jars of hope smashed, boxes of promise emptied, cartons of longing shaken, poured out, and crushed.

"My parents are dead." He repeated those words over and over. "Myparentsaredeadmyparentsaredeadmyparents-aredeadmyparentsaredead."

The Baron clapped his hands. If he had any sympathy for Bolt's grief, he did not show it. "You and I are together at last. Let the villagers fight. Let them fire the cata-pults. They will not stop us. No one can! Mwah-ha-ha . . . Ergh . . ." He coughed while laughing evilly. "Sorry, choked on a fish bone." He then let loose another evil laugh that was even more evil than all the others. "I will leave you with your thoughts." He strode toward the door. "I have but one rule, Humboldt. That you remain in this tower."

"You already have three other rules," Bolt reminded him, wiping the wet from his eyes. "There's the question rule and the villager rule, and also the stay-in-bed rule, but I'm guessing that's not really a rule anymore."

"Well, OK, so I have a few rules. Sue me." The Baron flicked the small cape on his back and it cracked like a whip. "I will see you tonight, Bolt. Soon, we celebrate."

The Baron marched through the door and slammed it behind him. Bolt heard the lock click, and when he rushed toward the door and tried to turn the knob, it didn't move.

Bolt rattled and banged the door, but it did no good. He crumpled to the floor and whimpered.

He had always insisted his parents had not abandoned him to an orphanage, even when no one would believe him. He had felt their love all the way down to his too-small-to-cover-his-ankles orphanage socks. But it didn't matter. They were not looking for him. He would never have a real family.

He was the chosen one—chosen to be unhappy, un-wanted, and unloved.

Meanwhile, brave Annika was a prisoner in the dun-geon, soon to be eaten by rats. All of Brugaria would soon be enslaved. Things couldn't get any worse.

A drop of water fell on Bolt's nose. Bolt looked up. Water dripped from the ceiling, possibly from a burst water pipe. *Drip, drip, drip.* Onto Bolt's nose.

OK, now things couldn't get any worse.

Bolt crawled off his bed, reached under his mattress, and grabbed the stuffed penguin that he had discarded two days before. The charcoaled fur around the missing wing took on a new, terrifying meaning. Bolt tore off the bird's head and then its one remaining wing, stuffing falling on the floor like fresh snow. Bolt tore out more of the penguin's cotton guts. He ripped the fabric and pounded his fist on the fluff around him, screaming as loud as he could.

Bolt stopped and stared at the shredded remains of Penguin. He grabbed fluff, cramming cotton into the torn spaces of the penguin, but it was like trying to put air back into a ripped balloon.

"I'm sorry, Penguin. I'm sorry," he muttered. Bolt stayed on the ground, sobbing, now more alone than ever.

33.
Another Penguin Night

Eventually, Bolt stopped sobbing. He sat on the bed trying to smooth his hornlike hair. The tufts wouldn't lie flat no matter how hard he licked his palms first. A cockroach hurried across the floor. If this were a fairy tale, the cockroach would talk. Maybe he and Bolt would sing a song about working and whistling. The bug would find a door key and free Bolt, who would discover his parents were alive.

This was no fairy tale. Bolt raised his foot to squash the insect, but then hesitated and watched it disappear behind the bookcase.

It wasn't the cockroach he wanted to smash, but the wretched Baron and his wicked plans and the empty feeling of helplessness that sat inside him under sooty layers of gloom.

Bolt walked to the window, his hands wrapped into fists and his fingers white from clenching. He stared out at the large, immaculate manor lawn, the forest surrounding it, and the waves, so far away. The penguin part of Bolt wanted to run along the shore and swim.

The human part of Bolt just wanted to smash these gray tower walls and find somewhere to wallow in his misery.

As he stared out the window, Bolt's eyes rested on the catapult. It sat on the roof beneath him, too far away to jump. Bolt wished he were a boulder, flung into space by that rooftop contraption.

If only he had never been sent here! If only he could sprout wings and fly away. He would sprout wings that evening, but he knew penguins could not fly.

As Bolt lingered at the window, he spied movement on the lawn. Bolt peered harder.

Frau Farfenugen hurried across the lawn in her combat boots, toward the tree line. The housekeeper twisted her head to the right and the left, but didn't think to look up to the tower. Another person emerged from the forest, a person almost twice her size.

The Fish Man.

The scar-faced giant held out his hands. The warty

and wrinkled Frau Farfenugen grabbed them. He pulled her close. They rubbed their noses together. And then, still holding hands, they dashed into the woods.

Bolt stepped back from the window, remembering the heart-covered letter Frau Farfenugen had dropped that morning. If the Baron discovered her romance, he would be very angry. He would probably turn his housekeeper into gum or caramel sauce, or hang her from a flagpole by her armpit hairs, or something else just as terrible.

Bolt grinned when he thought of armpit-hair hanging, and then shrank in terror. That momentary glee had been pure Baron: his evil thoughts still lingered inside Bolt.

Would Bolt soon be as evil as the beast that was responsible for his parents' deaths?

Bolt glanced at the penguin books on the shelf. He walked over and grabbed a book. Perhaps it would keep his mind from dwelling on his hopelessness and his Baron-influenced anger.

Bolt scanned through Volume I of the penguin encyclopedia. He read how penguins lived in colonies, called rookeries, which could number ten thousand penguins strong. He read how their feathers kept them warm. He learned how, despite not having visible ears, penguins had excellent hearing.

But what he found the most fascinating was what he

learned about penguin families. Unlike most other animals, many penguin species mated with each other for life. When an egg was laid, both penguins cared for it, and raised the chick together. These penguin chicks were never abandoned.

Even humans abandoned their kids, like so many of the boys back at Oak Wilt.

Bolt closed his eyes. He could feel a part of him, the penguin part, stirring inside him. And then he thought of something that would have seemed impossible before now, that would have seemed as strange as eating a live goldfish just two days ago:

Could a penguin family be a *real* family? Could they become Bolt's real family?

No. The thought was absurd. His depression was making him delirious.

Bolt slammed the book shut. He needed to get out. Hunt the Baron down. Avenge his parents. Save Brugaria.

Or, he needed to sleep. That sounded like a good plan, too. A wave of exhaustion swept over him. And when was the last time he had eaten anything? As suddenly as his tiredness came the hunger, a nearly insatiable desire for raw fish. He was so very hungry. And so very tired.

Hours later, Bolt was jostled awake by the chimes of the clock and a tingling feeling spreading through his body. It was deep into the night, and the moon cast its rays through the window. The clock chimes rang. It was midnight. The moment he feared most.

Bolt went to the window, and the full moon bathed him in light.

Bolt's body rippled, his feet turned orange, and he opened his mouth to scream.

Instead, he barked.

PART FOUR

The Attack of the Werepenguin

34.
Really? Another Break in the Action? This Is Getting Annoying.

As I stood at the St. Aves Zoo, the frigid night winds slammed against me like a ship smashing into an iceberg. The penguins chattered among themselves. I stifled a sneeze.

The penguin caretaker looked at me with a combination of pity and resignation, or perhaps a combination of revulsion and nausea, or a combination of patience and hypothermia, or perhaps none of those. Like a book without punctuation, he was hard to read.

"It is late," he said. "We should continue our story later. In the morning, perhaps, after a good night's rest."

I shook my head, both to show my disagreement with his terms, and also to shake off another sneeze threatening to shoot from my nostrils. "You will finish your story," I commanded. "I will catch the first boat home, your penguins in tow, assuming you keep your end of the bargain."

"I will not shirk from it. The penguins are yours if you want them," the man assured me. "I merely make the suggestion because of the time, and because your teeth are chattering."

"My teeth chatter from the night air, not from the fear of monstrous penguins. Horror stories will not change my mind. But I admit I have a new appreciation for those birds. Perhaps they deserve an exhibit as large and as comfortable as this one. I promise I will ship them to my zoo in a box made of extra-comfortable wood and I will personally add more airholes."

The man sighed, a loud sigh that reminded me more of a foghorn than a person breathing. It was so loud, even the penguins craned their necks to look.

"Very well," the man said. "But once again we need to take a slight detour to catch up on Annika and her—"

"I hate interruptions," I said with a frown.

35.

The Greatest Bandit Who Ever Lived

arlier that evening, while Bolt was in the tower and before midnight approached, Annika opened her eyes. She was alarmed to find herself sitting on the cold stone ground of a prison cell. One of her wrists was shackled to the wall by a chain. She yanked her arm, but the chain did not budge, and instead merely hurt her wrist.

The chain creaked as she yanked. It was old and rusted, but not so old nor so rusted that it broke.

Annika glared at the gray stone walls around her, grim and ragged. The cell had no chair. No bed. No toilet. There was a window, but it was small, covered with steel bars, and too high to reach. A sliver of moon glow peeked through.

There were also rats. She heard them chattering in the walls. One scurried across the floor, looked at her, and then slowly neared. Annika kicked at the rodent. It stepped back, shrugged, and ran away.

If it was looking for dinner, the rodent would need to wait until Annika was too weak or hungry to fight back.

Or maybe she should let the rat nibble on her. She probably deserved it. Annika hung her head in shame. First, the villagers had captured her to hang her, and now the Baron had defeated her with a penguin. Great bandits did not allow themselves to be captured even once, let alone twice in the same week.

Maybe she wasn't quite ready to be a bandit, like her father had said. Maybe, like blanched potatoes, she needed some seasoning.

She couldn't get any seasoning shackled in a basement, though. She would need to get out of there first.

Annika withdrew two bobby pins from her hair, rubbed them against her fingers, and then got to work. Winning the bandit lock-picking contest had been easier than picking this lock, though—the mechanism inside was old and rusted, and her rough tools had a hard time manipulating the parts inside.

After a few anxious moments, including twice when she feared one of her bobby pins would snap in two, and with her heart speeding faster and faster, Annika heard a faint *click*, and the lock popped open. Her racing heart slowed down to a trot.

She rubbed her wrist. Her skin felt raw where the shackle had squeezed. She stood up and walked to her door. As she expected, it was locked, but that didn't worry Annika much. Her bobby pins had proven to be strong.

She reached her thin arm through the bars of her cell and around to the lock. Less than a minute later she was creeping down the hallway.

As she crept, Annika glanced at another cell in the hallway, where a skeleton lay, chained to a wall. Whoever it was hadn't had a bobby pin.

Annika walked quietly. She didn't pass guards. She didn't hear the Baron. No one would notice she was gone except the rats.

The hallway led to a staircase, and at its top was a door that led directly to the lawn.

Annika opened the door and stared out at the great expanse of green grass mottled with white snow behind the manor. For a brief moment, she considered finding the tunnels and fleeing Brugaria to become the bandit she had always dreamed she would be. Then she would return, years later, triumphant and battle-tested, ready to take her place as the leader of the bandits. But now she could leave as easily as a cow could rob a carriage, which is to say, not easily at all. She had seen the Baron's twisted smile, filled with wickedness and malice. She had heard his evil plans.

If he wasn't stopped, no one was safe.

She stepped out the door of the manor when, somewhere, a grandfather clock chimed over and over again. Eleven times? No, twelve.

Wild penguin barking echoed across the land.

Above, the full moon shone. The echo of waddling feet grew closer. The forest itself seemed to come alive as ice cracked and the ground rattled.

A bush was next to her. Annika dove behind it, hiding from view, as an army of penguins trampled across the lawn. They looked wicked. Vicious.

Something bigger ran among them. The biggest penguin she had ever seen.

A werepenguin.

It was Bolt. She could see it in the penguin's eyes: a flicker of humanity. Annika stayed behind that bush, trembling, not daring to move, waiting for morning to come, hoping that, somehow, she could convince her family to fight this evil.

36.

A Light from the Darkness

The next morning, Bolt awoke on the floor of his room in a rather large puddle. His tuxedo, what little was not torn and ripped, dripped seawater. Fish bones lay on the floor.

He didn't remember very much about the previous night, and the few things he could piece together, he didn't like. He had chased people. He had smashed things. He had given someone a wedgie. The nighttime was penguin time.

Bolt remembered the seafood market. It had taken the worst of the nighttime attack as he and a gang of penguins broke windows to plunder a treasure trove of fish and seafood piled on buckets of ice. They also whittled their initials on the floor. They used the bathrooms and left the toilet seats up.

But the worst part of his memories?

He remembered enjoying all of it.

He had stood next to the Baron, too. Run with him. Swum with him. Bolt could have done something; he'd had plenty of chances. But the idea had not even entered Bolt's mind. Instead, he had obeyed the Baron willingly. Happily.

Bolt walked over to the closet and found the clothes he'd been wearing when he left the orphanage. They sat in a ball on the floor, damp and smelly, but Bolt put them on anyway. He already shared the Baron's ghostly pallor and penguin-like nose and hair tufts, but he didn't have to share the same wardrobe. He vowed he would never wear a tuxedo again.

He was putting on his shirt when the bookcase moved. Startled, Bolt jumped back. It inched forward farther. It squeaked, and then squawked. Bolt jumped in alarm.

The entire case slid over, and Annika entered the room, shaking snow from her shoes. The bookcase, it seemed, hid a secret stairway.

"What are you doing here?" Bolt asked, amazed.

"Freeing you."

"I would have freed you if I could have," said Bolt in an apologetic tone. "I thought about it. But I was sort of stuck up here."

"Didn't I tell you about the secret tunnels?" Bolt

nodded. "And how they were in lots of houses and building?" Bolt nodded again. "And to always check behind bookshelves?" Bolt shook his head. "Sorry, then. My bad."

"It's nice of you to rescue me, though."

"I'm not nice," said Annika, growling. She spoke in her best bandit voice, trying to sound both firm and cruel. "Bandits are not nice. I owe you one, that's all. I'm a ruthless bandit. Besides, I need you."

"I still think it's nice."

Annika kicked the floor and frowned. "Stop saying that. Now let's go. We need to get out of here."

"Out of Brugaria?"

"I've scrapped that plan. We're heading back to the forest. I need to convince my father of the Baron's plans and, well, one look at you, and he'll have to believe me."

Bolt glanced at his ghostly white reflection in the mirror. A shudder shot through him.

Annika waved Bolt to the bookshelf, but Bolt didn't move. "What are you waiting for? Your face isn't going to get any less penguin-like by looking at it. We need to warn my family."

Bolt sighed. He had never been cute or cuddly like so many other orphans, but now with his ashen face, his tufts of hair, and his slightly larger nose, his un-cute-ness and un-cuddly-ness were more obvious than ever.

But that night, he would look far worse. He would be a complete and total monster.

Bolt lifted his chin as he turned to Annika. "I can't go with you."

"You want to stay here?"

"No, I mean I can't go with you to the forest. I need to find Blazenda. She says I'm the chosen one."

"Chosen to do what?"

"To defeat the Baron and free the penguins, at least I think so. Honestly, no one seems to be completely sure. I could just be chosen to do his laundry, but that would be terribly anticlimactic." Annika opened her mouth to protest, but Bolt held his hand up. "If I go with you, I'll become a penguin again. I'll fight against you, and the Baron will be unstoppable, or so he says. I need to find Blazenda."

"That old fortune teller tried to hang me."

"I never said she was perfect."

"You can say that again."

"OK, I never said she was perfect." Annika threw Bolt a dirty look. "Blazenda told me that I had to free myself to free you all. Maybe it meant nothing. All I know is that I need to find out and do what I'm chosen to do."

"But why were you chosen? You're not mighty or brave."

"I didn't choose myself. This neck birthmark did. Maybe it knows something I don't."

Annika sighed, took out her knife, stared at the blade,

and then thrust it back into her belt. "I'm a horrible bandit," she groaned. "Fine. I'll help you find the Fortune Teller. You'd better be right about this. Now, let's get out of here." She paused and sneered. "And just so you know, this does not mean I'm nice. I'm still ruthless."

"Right. Ruthless. Got it." Softer, Bolt added, "But I still think you're nice."

Annika growled and then stepped toward the open space behind the bookcase, Bolt behind her. The door to the tower bedroom swung open with a rusty creak. Bolt and Annika turned, ready to fight.

Frau Farfenugen stepped into the room holding a platter of dead fish.

The lowly housekeeper dropped the platter in surprise. It clanged against the hard wooden floor. Frau Farfenugen pointed to Annika while shooting Bolt a withering glare. "I leave you alone and you sneak friends into your room? I'm very disappointed in you."

"My name is Annika Lambda and I'm the fiercest bandit in the world."

"Then why have I never heard of you before now?" The housekeeper's eyes narrowed.

Annika frowned and slumped her shoulders. "I'm working on that."

"She's very nice," said Bolt.

"No, I'm not," grunted Annika.

Bolt looked at the fish that had fallen from the tray onto the floor and was filled with a ravenous craving to eat. He dropped down to the ground and crammed halibut and minnows from the dirty floor into his mouth as fast as he could. So delicious! He savored each wet, rubbery carcass.

When Bolt saw the housekeeper and Annika staring at him, their mouths agape, he stopped eating and emitted a small burp. He blushed. "I guess I was hungry."

"Bolt and I are leaving," said Annika to the housekeeper. "He's going to save Brugaria. Or at least he'd better. And, hopefully, he'll learn how to use a fork and a napkin."

"I have to find Blazenda," added Bolt, wiping fish slime on his pants. "And yeah, a napkin would be nice."

Frau Farfenugen scowled. She backed up slowly to the door. "I have no napkins. Even worse, the Baron has threatened to sew me into mittens if the boy escapes again. I don't even like mittens. It's very hard to pick up small objects with them. Gloves are much better. But I shouldn't complain. I'm just a lowly housekeeper who doesn't deserve any hand-warming outerwear."

Annika bounded over to the housekeeper and held her knife to her throat. "Should I slit her throat?" she asked Bolt. "Just say the word."

"Really? Would you do that for me?" asked Bolt. He had never known anyone who would slit a throat for him before.

"No, probably not." She lowered her knife. "I'm a terrible bandit."

"You're still starting out," said Bolt. "I'm sure one day you'll be able to slit anyone's throat, anytime." Bolt now turned to the housekeeper, who was staring at the door as if planning to turn around and run. "Help us escape, or I'll tell the Baron about you."

The housekeeper eyed Bolt warily. "Tell him what?"

"About you and the Fish Man, and how you sneak out of the manor to see him. I spied you."

The housekeeper spat angrily on the ground. "I looked left and right when I ran out the other day, and forgot to look up. But you wouldn't tell the Baron."

"I would."

"He'd never believe you."

"He'll find your love letters."

Frau Farfenugen looked at the tray by her feet, the tray she had dropped and that held the dead fish, and sighed. "I should help you anyway. The Baron must be stopped." She pointed to the secret tunnel. "But I'm going with you. Maybe, just maybe, a lowly housekeeper such as I can find happiness, as improbable as that would seem. Although probably I'll just find misery and woe."

The three of them hurried toward the hole in the wall. They dashed down a dark spiraling staircase, through an ancient, crumbling hall, slid down a bumpy chute, and then rushed down a tunnel that was damp and cold, carved into the earth. Cracks from above provided fragments of sunlight, just enough for them to see where they were going.

The tunnel soon split into two, and Frau Farfenugen ran down the tunnel on the left. Annika pointed to the tunnel on the right. "This one leads back to town."

"Then where did Frau Farfenugen run to?"

"Who knows? The tunnels can get confusing. But we're going this way. I'm fast, so keep up."

Bolt wiggled his toes. He was wearing the shoes from the orphanage, if you could call them shoes. They were really just burlap sacks with laces. He couldn't run fast, but he needed to do his best. He was almost out of time.

He knew he might be Brugaria's only hope. The penguins' only hope. But, deep down, it all felt very, very hopeless.

37.

A Storm Approaches

After running, jogging, and dashing down a confusing maze of underground passages, Annika and Bolt scurried up a small ladder. They stood surrounded by endless rows of identical grave markers. Flowers lay on many of the graves, perhaps dropped by loved ones that very morning.

At the edge of the vast lawn were four tall stone penguin statues on high pedestals. Each penguin stood proud, posed in a stoic salute.

"Where are we?" Bolt asked, his voice swept away by the whistling wind.

"The penguin cemetery," said Annika. "Where the great penguins are buried, and the not-so-great penguins.

Really, they let in just about anyone, as long as it's a penguin."

"I guess everyone ends up in a graveyard eventually," Bolt said. "Unless you are cursed as a werepenguin for eternity. Then, maybe not." He looked down, sighed, and then looked up at the large statues. "Why are they saluting?"

"Who knows? They're just stupid statues. Everyone knows penguins don't salute. Come on. Cemeteries sort of creep me out."

Bolt followed Annika past the grave markers. Walking with Annika, a girl his age who sometimes did nice things for him although she insisted she wasn't nice, he could almost imagine a life that didn't end in horror.

Almost, but not entirely. Bolt was still pretty much convinced his life was going to end in horror.

"You know, you're the first real friend I've ever had," said Bolt.

Annika frowned. "We're not friends," she spat.

Bolt slowed and he kicked a rock. "But you saved my life and now you're going to help me find the Fortune Teller. That's pretty friendly."

Annika sighed and kicked another rock. "Fine. We're friends. Just don't tell anyone, OK? I have my reputation as a cruel bandit to think about."

They jogged a long way. Bolt was not used to jogging long distances, but running with a friend—his first real friend!—gave him energy he'd never imagined he had. Or maybe it was the penguin blood stirring inside him. Or both those things.

Large gray clouds filled the sky, blotting out the sun.

"Do you think it will be easy to break the curse and stop the Baron?" asked Bolt. "Some secret spell or something?"

"I have no idea. I'm not a fortune teller."

"But what if it's too hard? What if it's impossible? I know I'll probably always be unwanted. I've sort of accepted that, I guess. But what if I'm doomed to be a monster forever?"

"You might not always be unwanted." Annika threw him a smile, but one mixed with so much pity it looked a bit more sneer-ish than smile-ish. They walked in silence, Bolt's unanswered questions lingering in the icy air.

They soon arrived at the edge of the town. It was hard to believe this was the same village that had been so alive with music and laughter the day before. The souvenir stands were gone, as was the scaffolding in the town square. The only sound was the cold wind blowing through empty streets.

As they walked through the barren village, Bolt stared at the penguin signs hanging in front of every building, rocking back and forth in the wind. Beautifully painted, artistically designed, these penguins smiled with cheerful grins.

These were penguins in their natural, peace-loving state—not twisted with demands to wage war.

A few townspeople watched Bolt and Annika from windows, peeking through closed blinds. Every time Bolt turned to meet someone's gaze, the eyes would vanish back into an unlit room. The people seemed scared.

Up above, the skies turned darker, mauve and violet, and distant fearsome clouds flickered with lightning. The wind grew even windier. A storm was brewing, still far away, but when it hit, it would be terrible.

Bolt's penguin blood made him immune to the icy breeze, but he shivered anyway. It felt like the appropriate thing to do. Tumbleweeds blew down the street. That was odd, since there were no tumbleweeds in Brugaria. Still, they tumbled by.

Catapults sat on the roofs of the buildings, unused. Bolt remembered the dead fish flung from their powerful arms just yesterday, and his stomach growled hungrily. The fish were gone now. Bolt's stomach was disappointed.

"Do we have far to go?" Bolt asked.

"Not very," said Annika. "The Fortune Teller lives in the Old and Seedy Part of Town. It's past those buildings and then down the hill."

They turned the corner and saw, up ahead, a store in tatters, its front window shattered. Splintered wood and broken glass were sprayed over the sidewalk.

This felt familiar. A wave of recognition swirled inside Bolt's brain. Bolt had been here last night. He had helped destroy this seafood market. He had barked gleefully.

Annika and Bolt stood in the shadow of an awning as they stared at the scene. What looked like penguin prints remained on the sidewalk—dozens of them. Fish bones were everywhere. Bolt could almost taste the plump, delicious fish meat.

Two men stood in the middle of the mess. One of the men was Günter. The whale prince wore his robe, although the hood was lowered. He was still armed with his loaf of French bread. Bolt trembled at its crustiness.

The second man was younger and much wider. He had two teeth. Bolt recognized this man, too.

"Where are you going?" Annika hissed. Bolt slunk closer to the men. He wanted to hear their conversation. He wanted to know more about the damage around their feet, as guilt for his part in the store's destruction burped inside him.

A clap of thunder sounded from the distance. The clouds were moving quickly. The skies directly overhead looked increasingly threatening.

"Storm coming," said the younger man, scanning the skies.

"It is another sign, Franz," said Günter. "Ludwig is in the hospital after defending his seafood shop. One of the penguins even crept upstairs and pulled mattress tags off the bed. It all points to the way things were before, just as I warned."

"Maybe it was an accident. A few bad eggs."

"Eggs did not do this. No, fully hatched penguins performed these wicked deeds. Franz, you are always seeing the world sunny-side up. But this was how the Great Bird Battle began—with looting and terrorizing couples out on strolls. The penguins are getting their feet wet for something bigger."

"Penguins love getting their feet wet," agreed Franz.

"They want to rule us. They want our homes, our food, and to force us to sit on their eggs and bake them fish sticks. The Mystical Brotherhood of Whales, or Sisterhood of Whales, or whatever we are now, must fight for our freedom. If not—then you and I will fight alone!" He thrust his French bread in the air. "Are you with me?"

"Of course," Franz said. "Anything to stop would-be bowling penguins."

"It's them or us." Günter raised his fist. Bolt leaned forward, and his foot slipped on some stones. Hearing the noise, Günter and Franz turned.

"Who is there?" cried Günter, raising his bread.

Bolt lowered his head and turned to leave. "No one at all," said Bolt in a high, disguised voice. Unfortunately, Bolt did not have much practice disguising his voice.

"It's the Baron's boy!" cried Günter. "The whale hater! Spying on us again!"

"I'm just a harmless villager," called out Bolt, now walking away at a faster pace. "And I don't have anything against whales. Really."

"Capture him!" cried Günter.

Bolt ran. Günter and Franz chased him, screaming for Bolt's head.

"Blubber, blubber, blubber!" shouted Franz.

Wide, frightened eyes stared out from windows as Bolt raced through the streets. Bolt's burlap Oak Wilt shoes had poor traction on the icy ground. He slipped. Günter and Franz grew nearer.

Above, the clouds continued growing closer, too. Soon they would both gain: the attackers and their menacing bread, the storm and its dangerous skies.

Bolt stopped at the top of a steep hill, and a feeling surged inside him, a feeling of anger and hatred, and then a love of fish sticks, which he did his best to ignore. He turned and gnashed his teeth at his pursuers. "Who are you to stop me?" he howled.

Günter and Franz halted, looked at each other, and then at Bolt, as if uncertain what to do. Bolt stared back, hissing.

"He's cursed." Günter raised his loaf of French bread. "The Brotherhood must defend Brugaria!"

"Or the Sisterhood or something else," added Franz.

Bolt felt a hand grab his arm. Annika stood beside him. "What are you doing?" she asked.

"I'll whittle them into toothpicks and then pick their bones from my teeth! They are making me very angry. And they don't want to see me very angry!"

Annika gasped. "What are you talking about?"

Bolt gasped, too. As suddenly as it had coursed inside him, the alien craving for violence oozed out of Bolt. He stood, blinking, as scared of what he was becoming as he was of the two men who faced him. "Actually, I won't do that. I don't even know how to whittle."

"Then stop standing here and run!" Annika ordered, facing Günter and Franz. "I'll slow them down. Get help. The Fortune Teller is down the hill."

"But what if Blazenda can't help me?"

"Just pray she can."

Bolt stared at the hill, still shaking from the all-encompassing evil that had briefly overwhelmed him. The hill sloped down, steep and covered in a thin sheet of ice. At the bottom were trees and buildings that were smaller and shabbier than the buildings near where he stood. As Bolt looked, his instincts took over.

Bolt kicked his feet back, stomach out, and landed on the ground, belly first, like a penguin. He slid down the icy hill, gaining speed. The slush whipped through Bolt's hair as he plunged downward faster and faster.

Behind him, he heard Günter cry out, "You can flee but you'll never escape us, whale hater! The war begins tonight!"

38.
Forsooth, the Tooth!

Bolt zoomed like a greased toboggan. He reached the bottom of the hill but kept skidding, through the snow-spotted grass and into the deserted street below.

Finally, his momentum ceased. Bolt stood and wiped the snow from his jacket.

A wooden sign read *Old and Seedy Part of Town.* In smaller words was *Please forgive our seediness!*

True to the sign, the stores were older and significantly seedier than those at the top of the hill. The cobblestones on the road were cracked. Penguin pictures hung in front of stores, but were crudely drawn and colored outside the lines.

Above, the clouds grew darker. The storm would soon begin.

Up ahead, two rocking chairs creaked next to a small table in front of the worst-looking building on the block. The front door leaned off its hinges, barely attached to the frame. The wooden walls on the building seemed unbalanced. The place needed painting. And a new roof. And new walls. Actually, it would probably have been easier to just tear it down and start over.

A sign said *Fortune telling by a cackling fortune teller.*

One of the creaking rocking chairs was empty. In the other sat Blazenda. She wore her black wedding dress and floppy witch hat, as well as the chains around her neck holding their various charms and animal feet. Her chains still clanged like wind chimes, although this time they played "Yankee Doodle Dandy." She napped, or maybe she was dead. Either way, she was still, her eyes closed. Bolt approached warily. "Hello?" he whispered. "Strange, disturbing fortune teller? Hello?"

He stood only a few feet away. The Fortune Teller had not yet moved, and whether or not she was breathing was difficult to tell. Bolt reached over to poke her. His finger crept toward Blazenda's shoulder.

Poke.

Before Bolt could move his finger away, the Fortune Teller grabbed his hand, and her eyes popped open. Bolt had forgotten how quick she was, and how powerful her grip. He grimaced as her nails dug deep into the flesh of his palm.

"Never awaken a sleeping fortune teller," said Blazenda, growling.

"I need your help," said Bolt.

"Of course you do," the Fortune Teller hissed. "I knew you would come." Above, thunder clapped and lightning cracked. "The storm is coming."

"It's still a bit far off," said Bolt.

"Not that storm, fool!" barked the Fortune Teller. "The storm inside your soul. The storm of penguins and the evil of the night!" She cackled.

"Really?" said Bolt. "Do you have to cackle all the time? It's still a bit creepy."

She released her grip and waved toward the chair next to her. "Sit. I will tell your fortune, without cackling."

"I don't need my fortune told. I need to know how to stop the Baron and my curse. You told me to come to you. I'm here. Tell me what to do. Save me."

"You must save yourself. Sit." The Fortune Teller stabbed her finger at the empty chair across from her. Bolt sighed, but did as he was told. The Fortune Teller looked down at the animal-tooth necklace around her neck and rubbed it gently. With a deep breath she removed a pack of Brugarian tarot cards hidden within the folds of her dress, and placed them on the table. She spread four cards face-down in front of her and turned the first one over.

On the card was a picture of a herring.

"The herring stands for possessions," said the Fortune Teller. "Someone wants to keep you in their power like a herring being eaten."

Bolt licked his lips. Herring made him hungry. Blazenda turned over another card. The word *Uno* was on it.

"Sorry, that's from the wrong deck."

She turned over the third card.

"The penguin. The mightiest of the cards. It means you are strong and meant to rule. Or it means you like to eat fish sticks. So, at least one of those two things."

She turned over the fourth card. It read *Deth*.

"Deth?" asked Bolt. "What's that?"

The Fortune Teller cackled. "It means you face certain death, boy!"

"But that's D-e-a-t-h. This just says D-e-t-h."

Blazenda picked up the card and stared at it. "You're right. It's probably just a mistake. I think it's supposed to be death, as in dying. You're going to die."

"Or it could be deth."

"Yes, you're right." She tossed the card over her shoulder, stood up, and shook her finger at Bolt. "No matter. You are cursed! Cursed by the moon! Cursed to live the rest of your life as a werepenguin! Cursed to follow the Baron's evilness forever! Unless . . ."

"Unless . . . ?"

The woman smiled and chanted.

"When the moon is high, beware the mark,
Where danger lurks and penguins bark.
For you shall change, you shall transform,
When penguin spirit inside is born."

Bolt stared at Blazenda. "I know that already, and the second verse, too. We're way past that."

The Fortune Teller nodded. "But you may not know this part—

Before three days and three nights are done,
'Fore change's course has ceased its run,
There is one truth: Impale the tooth!
And freedom will be won."

"OK, I don't know that part," admitted Bolt.

"It's from the extended dance mix. The meter is slightly off, and few know it."

"But what do those lyrics mean?" asked Bolt.

"Must I spell it out for you, boy?"

"Actually, yes."

"Y-O-U M-U-S-T . . ."

"What are you doing?"

"Spelling it out."

"Just say it without being so confusing, please."

"Fine," she said with a sigh. "But it takes all the fun out of things. You must find the werepenguin that bit you within three days of being turned and then, at night, while the creature turns into a penguin, stab him with the tooth of a killer whale. The curse will then be lifted, the werepenguin destroyed, and the penguins freed. Simple as pie."

Bolt stared at Blazenda. And then he stared longer. "Three days?"

"Yes, three days."

"How is that simple as pie?"

"Because pies are actually quite difficult to make."

"I don't get it."

Blazenda growled. "Pay attention. While the Baron transforms into a penguin, but before he does completely, you must stab him with a killer whale tooth. What part don't you understand?"

"Everything!" cried Bolt. "How am I supposed to do that? There must be another way."

"Why must there be?"

"OK. I suppose there mustn't, necessarily. Has anyone ever succeeded in breaking the curse and slaying a werepenguin?"

"Not that I know of."

"Then how can you be sure that it will work?"

"I'm not. People aren't turned into werepenguins every day, you know. But at least it is a chance. What other option do you have?"

Bolt gulped. He needed to confront the Baron tonight, at exactly the stroke of midnight, and kill him, all while he was also turning into a penguin at the same time. How was that even possible?

"Remember," said Blazenda. "Only you can stab him and no one else or your curse will remain. And it must be from a killer whale's tooth, not any other weapon, or the curse will remain forever."

"What if I stab him but then someone else kills him?"

"Still cursed."

"Someone else stabs him and I kill him by chopping off his head?"

"Still cursed."

"I stab him with a tooth at the exact same time someone else chops off his head?"

"I have no idea. You got me on that one."

That didn't help very much, since Bolt couldn't possibly imagine any of those things happening. "Where can I find a killer whale's tooth?" he asked, but he already knew the answer.

The Fortune Teller grabbed the tooth necklace on the chain around her neck, lifted it off, and placed it around Bolt's neck. "Take the tooth. Unless you know of a good whale dentist?" Bolt shook his head. "Then take mine."

Bolt felt the tooth's sharp edge. A drop of blood emerged from his finger where he pricked it.

"The tooth is the Baron's only weakness. Now go! May you end the curse. For yourself, and for all of us!" She cackled but then Bolt threw her a dirty look. "Sorry, bad habit." She put her hand on Bolt's shoulder. "One final word. The curse comes from the moon. You can only transform when it shines."

"And how does that help me?"

"I don't know. It probably doesn't help at all. I just wanted to give you a final word."

Bolt stood up from the creaky chair and walked out to the street. He wandered aimlessly, plodding forward, barely paying attention to the shabby buildings he passed. So many people were counting on him, and for what? For him to do the impossible? Bolt pushed the thought away, but other thoughts flowed in.

Was the housekeeper safe?

Had Annika escaped the whale folk?

Had his orphanage pants shrunk? They felt tighter than usual, and it made wandering aimlessly quite uncomfortable.

The wind picked up and the clouds plunged the world into an even more despairing dimness. Bolt stumbled from the cold gale beating against him. It grew so dark, it almost looked like night. The thunder rumbled and lightning snapped its electrical tentacles. Strangely, more tumbleweed blew.

Bolt trembled. He was not brave or mighty. He was not a thunderbolt. He was just a boy who liked to bolt from danger.

Why did he think he could ever be anything else?

If the Brugarians and the penguins were counting on Bolt to save them, then they had better also be counting on despair, gloom, and living the rest of their lives under the Baron's ruthless control.

39.
Brothers in Arms, or Fins

As Bolt stumbled forward, lightning flashed in the distance and thunder rumbled closer. But Bolt was barely aware of the sky. He was barely even aware of where he was walking, and strolled into a tree. He rubbed his nose, and then veered left, now paying a little more attention to where he walked.

But he had so many more things to worry about than walking into trees, and so little time to do it. Midnight came nearer every second.

Nearer.

Nearer.

Nearer.

Although it was dark, violent flashes of light filled the too-close stormy skies and peeled the blackness back, revealing gray and violet clouds. A soft snowfall began, a few flakes, but a sign of things to come.

Up ahead, through the gloom, Bolt spied a small group of penguins huddled together. He could feel their angry and hate-filled thoughts. As Bolt grew closer, he saw they were rummaging through something.

It was a bowling-ball bag, and Bolt assumed they had stolen it. One of the birds was trying to slip into a pair of shoes, but his webbed feet were too big. Another penguin kept trying to pick up the ball, but it was too heavy. Another penguin pecked at a bag of food on the ground. The bag read *Flounder Chips.* Bolt's stomach growled in hunger, but his eyes flashed with anger at the scavenging beasts.

"That's not yours!" shouted Bolt. "Shoo. Get!" He had no patience for these penguin ruffians. They scowled back at Bolt. He reached inside their addled, rotten brains. He had spoken to a single penguin at the festival, ordering it to attack. Could he control an entire group? *I said get! Go!*

The group hissed, but obeyed. They scurried off, one grabbing the bowling shoes and one pushing the ball, rolling it in front of them.

One of the birds remained. It looked up from the flounder chips it had been eating and stared at Bolt.

"I said get out of here! You and your kind aren't in control yet. I can stop you, maybe. It's quite doubtful, to be honest. But that's beside the point. Scram!"

The penguin was shorter than the other penguins Bolt had seen, and fluffier. This bird was younger—not a child, but not yet an adult, either.

This penguin's mind was less coated with anger than that of the others. The Baron's evil thoughts were there: that dark wall of hatred storming inside the bird's brain was pure Baron. But there was something else. Friendliness? Innocence?

Hope?

Perhaps the Baron's dark presence was not as strong as Bolt feared. Where there were a few untainted thoughts, there must be more. Perhaps the other penguins had not completely gone to the dark side, either.

Perhaps twisted penguin brains could still be untwisted.

Bolt knew, then and there, why he was the chosen one.

He had been chosen because of his talent, and it wasn't a talent to sing or know state capitals, but the talent to be a penguin. To understand penguins. To understand the importance of family.

All his life, Bolt had known that his real family was waiting for him. And it was true. He had just been imagining the wrong family. *This* was his family, and it always had been.

Bolt had to break his curse or the penguins might never be saved. But if he broke his curse, he would no longer be a penguin.

He shook his head at the irony. He had finally found his real family. And the only way to save them could be to lose them.

The younger penguin waddled up to Bolt. The bird stared at him, its mind confused. It poked Bolt with its wing. *Are you our BFF?*

Bolt laughed. "No." He rested his hand on the bird's shoulder. "I'm your brother."

The penguin put its flipper around Bolt, and hugged him. *Brother.*

Bolt stood, feeling awkward, his orphanage clothes growing damper from the wet, clammy penguin hugging him. But Bolt returned the hug. He couldn't remember ever hugging someone before, or being hugged.

He had a lot to learn about having a family. It was too bad he might never have time to learn it.

After hugging for a few moments, Bolt gently nudged the penguin away. Above, the thick clouds continued to gather, and the clock crept closer to sundown, and midnight.

He needed to march to the manor.

The penguin followed him.

"Stay here," Bolt said to the bird, waving his hands and stomping forward. The penguin stomped toward him. "I said stay. You understand? I have to do this myself." The penguin nodded.

Bolt marched three steps forward and turned his head to see the penguin marching three steps toward Bolt. "I mean it. Don't follow me." Bolt plodded four steps forward. The penguin plodded four steps closer. Bolt hopped two steps. The penguin hopped two steps. Bolt pranced six steps ahead, while spinning. The penguin pranced six steps toward Bolt, and spun, despite the trickiness of prancing and spinning with webbed feet.

"Oh, come on. Now you're just doing that to be annoying." Bolt moaned. "I mean it. I must do this on my own."

Loud barking echoed in the distance. More penguins, angry penguins, were out there, calling their brethren to join them.

A cry for war.

It would start tonight unless Bolt was successful in his mission.

The penguin twisted its head toward the sounds. Bolt dashed away, and this time the penguin did not follow.

Now Bolt walked forward, not aimlessly but with purpose. The penguin barks faded. He needed to find the Baron. For his brothers. For his family.

Up ahead, the statues of the four saluting penguins rose in their proud, stony glory. Bolt was back in the penguin cemetery. A flash of lightning lit the dark day, unveiling a person standing by a tombstone amid the penguin statues. Another lightning bolt revealed the back of Frau Farfenugen. The lowly housekeeper wore a thick wool coat.

Bolt approached her, and at the sound of his footsteps, she wheeled around. When she saw it was Bolt, she bowed. Her mouth turned up in an odd smile, as if she knew a secret.

"Why are you smiling?" asked Bolt.

"No reason." She stopped smiling, and pointed to the sky. "Storm coming."

"I've heard that."

Thunder boomed and, just then, the sky cracked. The flakes that a moment before were sprinkling down became a blanket so thick it turned the world white.

"Never mind. Storm's here," said Frau Farfenugen. Bolt kicked his shoes, already covered in white fluff. He had never seen such rapid snowfall, although it didn't slow the thunder and lightning that sizzled all around them. Lightning and snow. Thunder snow.

A fresh bouquet of flowers lay on the ground at the grave marker next to them, although it was already covered in white. "I didn't take you for a penguin lover," said Bolt. "Whose grave are you visiting?"

"See for yourself," croaked Frau Farfenugen, her voice quivering.

The enormous flakes had already obscured the marker,

so Bolt had to bend and wipe off the snow with his hand. He leaned down to see the writing on the stone.

The marker was blank.

"I don't understand," said Bolt.

Frau Farfenugen buried her head in her hands. She might have been sobbing, but through the sheets of snow, it was impossible to tell. Her voice broke in a wail of despair. "This grave is my mother's!"

"Why is her grave unmarked?" Then he gasped. "Was—was your mother a penguin?"

"Of course not," snapped Frau Farfenugen. "How would that even be possible? Do I have a beak? My mother was the Baron's housekeeper before me. If I stayed with the Baron, my eternal reward would be an unmarked grave in a penguin cemetery, too. I will have a different future even if, as a lowly housekeeper, I deserve nothing but misery." She shivered. "And I'm terribly sorry about your head." She smiled again, the same knowing smile.

Bolt narrowed his eyes, confused. "What about my head?"

She ran her fingers through her hair, tapping her head and grimacing. "It can't feel much worse than someone slamming a tray of dead fish on your head."

"What do you mean?"

Bolt saw something flying toward his head; it might have been an apple.

Then he felt no more.

40.

If You Listen Carefully, You Can Hear Nothing

Before an apple hit his cranium, before Bolt wandered into the graveyard, before he accepted his fate as the chosen one and embraced the penguins as his real family, in fact even before he met with the Fortune Teller, he had left Annika to face the Prince of Whales and Franz by herself.

Annika stood before them, holding her knife.

"Go away. We want the whale-hating boy, not you," growled Günter.

"I'm going nowhere. Bolt is our only hope to save all of Brugaria," said Annika. "And I'm pretty sure he doesn't hate whales."

"You must think I was born yesterday," yelled Günter, jabbing his bread at Annika. "What day is it?"

"Sunday," said Franz.

"Then Saturday. You must think I was born Saturday."

"I was born on a Saturday," said Franz. "Not yesterday. But a while ago."

"I've never thought about what day you were born," said Annika. "I promise."

"You lie!" cried Günter.

Annika might not have been the greatest bandit, not yet anyway, but she was the fastest bandit, so she crossed the ground quickly. The menacing sky had not yet shed its first snow, but the ground was still slippery, and ice crunched under her feet as thunder roared in the distance.

She hurled her knife toward the weathered whale prince. Her knife-throwing pillow practice came in handy as her weapon sailed swiftly and surely. But the whale prince was no pillow. Günter parried with his French bread. The knife sank deep into its crust and stuck in place.

Annika groaned, and then jumped back as Günter rushed forward, waving his stale bread loaf.

Annika was not only quick but also nimble. She would have jumped over candlesticks easily. She ducked, and the loaf missed her head by inches. She danced back, out of the whale prince's reach, while slipping the bobby pin from her hair. It wasn't much of a weapon, but bandits often had to make weapons from ordinary objects.

Naturally, some ordinary objects made better weapons than others. Irons, for example. Irons made great weapons. Hammers, rakes, and various household poisons could also be quite handy in a fight, the latter if you were serving dinner.

But bobby pins? If Annika had been allowed to attend Felipe's weekly Making Weapons from Ordinary Objects

bandit classes, held right after knife-throwing practice, she would have known that bobby pins made awful bandit weapons, along with postage stamps, toenail clippings, and pianos. Pianos were far too heavy to hoist while fighting.

So, clueless, Annika leapt into the air, her bobby pin in her hand. Günter guffawed at the weapon, swiftly twirled his French bread, and swatted her away. The bobby pin sailed into a bush.

Annika flew back, too. Before she could plop onto the ground, arms grabbed her from behind.

Annika thrashed, but Franz was as strong as he was wide. He lifted her into the air, her legs kicking.

Kicking legs can be dangerous, as Franz learned when Annika's heel crashed into his kneecap. Franz's knee buckled, and Annika, free from his grasp, performed three quick aerials backward. Her gymnastic performance surprised even her.

"I give you an 8," said Günter, clapping.

"I say a 7.5," said Franz, also clapping while hopping on one leg.

"I thought it deserved at least a 9," said Annika, frowning.

The Prince of Whales held his French bread loaf over his shoulder, wiggling it like an anxious baseball batter. "You're quick and nimble, but you don't stand a chance against my French bread."

"Let's make her our prisoner," said Franz.

"No, I'll knock her out with my bread," countered Günter.

"Prisoner!" shouted Franz.

"Bread!"

"Prisoner!"

"Bread!"

"How about if you hit her with your bread and then we keep her prisoner?" suggested Franz.

Günter shrugged. "I can live with that."

While crouching, Annika held her hands out in fists. She didn't need a weapon to fight these men. The greatest bandit who ever lived didn't need a weapon to fight anyone. "Bring it on," she hissed.

As Günter straightened, his eyes blinked. His finger pointed. Franz's mouth opened wide, and a whimper trickled out.

Then, they turned and ran.

"We will be back," shouted Günter. "The war starts tonight."

Annika stood up straight, scratching her head as the two men disappeared around a corner. She licked her thumb, which had a slight cut on it. "Wow, I really am a great bandit," she muttered to herself. She couldn't believe she had scared them away. She only regretted her father had not seen her victory.

"We've been looking all over for you," said her father. "We thought you might have run away."

Annika turned. Her father stood behind her, along with Felipe and six other forest bandits. That was why the whale men had run. "We were watching," said Felipe. "You showed real bravery."

Annika kicked the snow, and her face flushed. "Ah shucks, I didn't do anything."

"You stood your ground. That's the first step," said Vigi Lambda. He smiled. Was it a smile of pride? He seemed to stand a little taller. "You shouldn't have tried to use a bobby pin, though. Maybe I should let you attend the next Making Weapons from Ordinary Objects class. You'll also learn that postage stamps, toenail clippings, and pianos make poor weapons. Pianos are just too heavy."

"I sometimes fight with pianos," said Brutus, the tallest and strongest of the bandits.

"But what are you doing here? Where have you been?" Vigi asked his daughter.

"I planned to run away, but I was captured, and then I was going to be hanged but I escaped, and then the Baron caught me and I escaped again, and then I was going to head back home but the whale folk tried to stop me. It's been a long couple of days. But more importantly, the Baron has prepared the penguins for war. He's going to attack. We need to fight him."

Her father frowned. "We have a truce."

Annika clasped Vigi's hand. "He'll never respect it, Papa. He'll turn on us. We need to battle."

"We will do no such thing," said Vigi. He stomped his foot on the ground. "It's too dangerous. I will not put my men at risk. I will not put my daughter at risk. Besides, there's no war coming. Those are just rumors because the Baron is so disturbing and discombobulating. I know there have been a few harmless penguin attacks, but that means nothing."

"That's how the Great Bird Battle began a hundred years ago," said Annika.

"Nonsense. Do you have proof he plans to start a war?"

Annika's shoulders slumped. She loved her father, but she hated his stubbornness. Bolt was her proof—if he were here, her father would have to believe her. But without her penguin-transforming friend—and she had to admit, they were friends—she would never convince the bandits to take up arms against the Baron.

Head down, she followed her father and the bandits back through the forest and toward the bandit campsite. It was all up to Bolt now.

All their lives were in his hands.

She just hoped he would have hands to save them, and not penguin wings.

41.
A Housekeeper Adrift

Annika and the bandits trudged through the forest. Most forest trudgers would have found the path too dark and desolate to follow. But the bandits knew the way well. A gnarled knot on a tree told them to turn left. A bush with black, poisonous berries meant they needed to go straight for twenty paces and then turn right. A dead duck, or at least a rubber duck that looked like a dead duck, was their cue to duck under a tree branch.

Rustling up ahead startled them. Instinctually Annika stopped, ready to run. A bandit was always ready to run from rustling. The leaves of a bush moved. Annika bounced on the soles of her feet. A bandit was always ready to bounce away from bush moving. A loud *THUD* followed, the sound of a head hitting a branch, and then an "Ow! My head!" from someone who did not know the duck meant to duck.

Annika stopped bouncing. Bandits did not flee from someone hitting a branch with their head.

Brutus and Felipe vanished into the forest, their years of banditry letting them step lightly and soundlessly. The forest was dark, so Annika could not see the commotion that followed, only hear it. There was a scream of surprise, a mild scuffle, a "Come now!" from Felipe, and a moment later they returned, Brutus's hand wrapped around the arm of Frau Farfenugen.

"Who are you?" Vigi demanded.

"Just a lowly housekeeper," she said, falling to her knees.

"She works for the Baron, or at least she did," said Annika, stepping forward. .

Frau Farfenugen shook her head and scowled, deeply. "I never worked for him. I was his prisoner. Have mercy on me."

Vigi stared at her, his lips pursed. "We'll return you to the Baron. If the rumors are true"—he glanced at Annika—"then we need to do whatever we can to be on the Baron's good side. What better way to seal our pact than to return his runaway housekeeper?"

Frau Farfenugen recoiled at the words. A look of dismal despair cast a shadow over her face. "Return me? You mustn't! You couldn't! You shouldn't!"

"Why notn't?"

Annika grabbed her father's arm. "She helped me escape, Papa. We should let her go."

Vigi frowned. "Bandits never show mercy."

"You're right. Never mind." To herself, Annika muttered, "I have so much to learn before I can be the greatest bandit who ever lived."

The housekeeper wept, and the tears rolled down her wart-dotted face and dripped off into the dirt beneath her. "Let me tell you my story," she begged. "Perhaps then you will decide to spare me."

"That seems unlikely," said Vigi. "But go ahead. I've never minded a nice story every now and then." From up above lightning flashed and thunder boomed. "But be quick. A storm's coming."

"Thank you," said the housekeeper. "I only hope a lowly housekeeper like me can deliver such a tale. It's a love story, of sorts. My mother fell in love, you see. Often, that is the start of a happy tale. Other times it is not, such as when a princess falls in love with a frog, but instead of it transforming into a prince with a kiss, it is merely a frog, and the princess has to marry a frog."

"So this is a story about a frog?" asked Vigi Lambda. He looked unimpressed.

"No, it is merely my introduction. May I continue?" When Vigi did not object, the lowly housekeeper told her story.

42.

The Final Break in the Action, We Promise

It was late, too late. The penguins in the exhibit here at the St. Aves Zoo looked as annoyed as I. They kept rocking back and forth, their webbed feet squeaking like a handful of cat toys.

"These constant stories within a story are bothersome," I said.

The penguin caretaker at the St. Aves Zoo sighed. "Some rugs are woven from one end to the other in a straight path, but others are woven in different pieces and then assembled. I'm afraid our tale is a rug like that. Let us take a moment to hear the housekeeper's story."

"Must we?"

"Let's. It's an interesting yarn."

I took a deep breath. "Hurry on with it, then. But it's late. I hope your story is almost done." The man nodded. "About time."

"Perhaps. But when we reach the end, you may wish we had never arrived."

43.
The Story of the
Lowly Housekeeper's Mother

Frau Farfenugen's mother, before she became Frau Farfenugen's mother, was a bright and spirited eighteen-year-old. Some said she was the most beautiful girl in all of Volgelplatz. At the annual Day of the Penguin Ball, forty-four young men asked her to be their penguin. There were only thirty-eight young men in town. A few asked her twice.

But her heart belonged to another. He was poor, with few earthly possessions. But he had one important one: he owned Frau Farfenugen's mother's heart. Some said that made him the richest person in Brugaria. Most wouldn't say that, but some people did. The two decided to run away. Elope. It was the only way they could be together. Her father disapproved of their marriage.

Although she loved the boy, the new bride also missed her home. She wished she had told her father the truth. She had married a flutist, even though her parents always hoped she would marry someone who played a stringed instrument.

Then, one day, her beloved's flute was stolen. She traveled late into the night to reach her parents' cottage so she could ask her father for help. Maybe he would take them in, teach her beloved to play another musical instrument, and then she wouldn't have to sleep in dirt every night or own just one shoe. She didn't tell her new husband she was leaving. Although poor, he was proud and would not want her father's help. So she went alone while her husband slept.

The reception was not a happy one.

"A flutist? Have you gone mad?" her father bellowed, his face turning red. "I will never let him set foot in this house."

"You'll feel differently when you meet him," the new bride insisted. "He's poor and has no schooling, but he's polite. We have an apple, too."

"Silence!" her father shouted. "You could have married a cello player. Get out!"

"But, Father, I'm still your daughter. It's not like he plays the trumpet."

"Don't ever say that word in this house." Her father's eyes bugged so far, they almost popped completely out of his head. "I never want to see you again. Go to your flutist. You've made your bed—now lie in it."

"Actually, we're poor and don't own a bed, which is one of our problems. Mother, surely you won't turn me away."

Frau Farfenugen's mother faced the woman who had stood silent all this time, her arms crossed. "Your father has spoken. Even a banjo-playing husband would have made us proud. Leave now. But stay on the main road. There are evil things that roam the woods at night. We may disown you, and never see or speak to you again, but that doesn't mean we don't care."

"It sounds like you don't care."

"Well, stay on the main road anyway, if you know what's good for you."

The new bride ran out of the house, tears of sadness and distress spraying from her like water from a lawn sprinkler. She didn't pay attention to where she fled—she merely ran and ran some more, which was impressive since she wore only one shoe. She didn't heed her mother's warnings about staying on the road, and soon found herself deep within the forest.

She saw light. She stepped through the trees and onto the vast lawn of Chordata Manor. She thought of the stories she had heard about it—terrifying tales of the supposed birdmen and monsters that lurked within. Rumors, probably, since no one ever dared visit the place. Still, she knew to keep away. She turned to head back into the forest and continue her crying and aimless running somewhere else.

"Wait." A boy, about twelve years old, stood only a few feet away. He was dressed in tuxedo pants, a white shirt, and a black cape sewn from penguin feathers. "You seem upset. Is everything OK?" He smiled and had dimples. Despite a disturbing, nearly pure white face, he appeared to be friendly, as dimpled people often are.

"My father has disinherited me. Our flute has been stolen. I only have one shoe. And I forgot to take money out of my dirndl pocket before I did the wash last week." She held up a small ball of crumpled paper. "See? Ruined."

"I have a flute. Would you like it?" asked the boy, smiling. "Perhaps some tea would perk you up, too. Care to go inside?"

The woman laughed. So this was the place everyone was so scared of—with a boy in a cape who made tea? And he had a flute, too! Relieved, she followed him inside. But once there, he slammed the door shut and locked all thirteen bolts and latches.

"I need a housekeeper," he said. "You shall be mine."

"You promised me a flute."

"I have none. I only have a banjo and a cello."

"Oh, if only I had fallen in love with someone like you,"

the new bride said softly. She shrugged. "Never mind. But I need to leave. My beloved is waiting for me."

"Never! I have only one rule. That you are my house-keeper and that you never leave."

"That's two rules."

"Fine, whatever. I am your master now."

"Give me a break!" she exclaimed, laughing. The new bride wasn't a naturally fearful woman. Someone doesn't sleep in dirt with a flute player and run around wearing one shoe if they are easily scared. "You're only a boy."

"Looks can be deceiving. I know the truth. I know that you eloped and that your father is not happy."

"How did you learn all that?"

"The penguins tell me everything."

The woman scoffed. "Penguins? Ha!" She laughed again for emphasis. "Ha! I'm leaving and you can't stop me."

"If you leave, I will hunt you down and fry your spleen in a sauté pan, as well as that of your family, your friends, and your husband."

"You wouldn't."

"Try me. I have a brand-new sauté pan, too."

She could see in his glowing red eyes that he spoke the truth. She would soon learn of his temper, and his insatiable appetite for power and for fish. She stayed—what other choice did she have?

After a month, the woman discovered she was pregnant, a lasting reminder of her brief but happy marriage.

And so a child was born, raised by her mother in between waiting hand and foot on the Baron, and sometimes wing and foot.

But one night, Frau Farfenugen's young mother decided she needed to try to escape, if not for her own sake, then for her child's. With her daughter by her side, she packed their things in a large brown sack. She crept out of the house, hoping to find her betrothed, whom she still loved, and maybe even her long-lost shoe.

But she didn't get far. She had not even made it into the forest when a band of penguins spotted her. The Baron appeared—not as a boy, but as a penguin. An evil penguin with horns and bushy eyebrows.

The woman and her daughter were trapped, and the Baron was angry. Very angry.

The woman begged for the Baron to spare her daughter's life. The Baron laughed and then ate the woman, or at least all of her except her bones, which he spat out.

But he spared the child. He said he needed a new housekeeper. So he buried the mother's skeleton in an unmarked penguin grave, and her daughter became the Baron's only servant.

44.
Reunited

While she told her story, Frau Farfenugen
had not looked up. Her eyes had remained
fixed on her gnarled, warty hands. And so
she did not notice Vigi's face growing paler and paler, his
arms and legs trembling, and his teeth nibbling his lips.
Annika noticed these things, but she did not understand
why they were happening.

When Vigi spoke, his voice quivered as much as his
limbs. "Was—was your mother's name Marcella?"

The housekeeper looked up then, and her eyes locked
with Vigi's, and a light seemed to shine in the dismal forest. Someone farted, but that only interrupted the mood
for a moment. Vigi swooped Frau Farfenugen into his

arms. "My daughter!" he cried, and he wept, and Frau Farfenugen wept and so did the bandits, Felipe loudest of all. No one cared that crying was forbidden by the Code of the Bandit except during a hanging, because only Vigi and Annika had actually read the code.

"Annika, meet your sister," said Vigi, choking on the tears that rained down his cheeks. "She looks just like her mother."

"But Frau Farfenugen is greenish, wart-covered, and half your height," said Annika.

"She has her mother's elbows."

Annika embraced her sister, and the three of them embraced one another, and soon Felipe and Brutus and all the other bandits were hugging them, too, creating a very large huddle of ten people until Frau Farfenugen piped, "I can't breathe!" and the group eased off.

The adopted daughter of Vigi Lambda looked at the slightly green, warty face of her newly discovered sister. She looked at her father. She looked back at the housekeeper's wrinkled cheeks. "Wait. How old are you?"

"Nineteen," wheezed Frau Farfenugen. She fluffed her hair. "But I've always looked mature for my age."

"Just a little," Annika agreed.

Vigi took his oldest daughter's hands in his. "You will live with us, of course. I will protect you. Nothing is more important than family. Although kidnapping and robbing carriages are only slightly less important."

"A lowly housekeeper like me does not deserve such happiness."

"You will never again be known as a lowly housekeeper," promised Vigi, staring into his daughter's eyes. "Instead, you will be known as a lowly former housekeeper."

"Oh, thank you, Daddy!" she cried.

"But what of the Baron?" asked Felipe. "He won't be pleased his housekeeper has escaped his manor to come live with you."

Vigi scowled. "I'll think of something."

"There's nothing to think about," said Annika. "We need to fight the Baron. Now more than ever."

Vigi stomped his foot. "No. I've already told you, we can't risk it. He's too powerful. I need to keep my daughters safe."

"But he already captured me once. He even imprisoned and ate your wife," protested Annika.

"No one's perfect," admitted Vigi Lambda.

"But you just told me that nothing is more important than family."

"Don't forget kidnapping and carriage robbing are important, too," Vigi noted. "But you are right. Family is everything: you, my new wart-covered daughter, and even the bandits. I love you all."

Felipe, Brutus, and many of the other bandits blushed. "We love you, too," Felipe blurted.

"That's why I can't fight him," continued the bandit

leader. "Revenge is only sweet if you win—otherwise the taste is very sour." The words were wise, although Annika noticed her father was sucking on a lime cough drop at that very moment. "My fighting him will not bring back my beloved Marcella. What's done is done."

Up above, thunder shook the air, and the first signs of snowfall fell above them, with a few flakes sneaking down from the canopy of tree branches overhead. "Let's head back to camp," Vigi added. "There's a storm coming."

Annika stepped in front of her father. If she was to be the greatest bandit who ever lived, she needed to do more than pick locks and rob carriages. She needed to lead and argue for what she believed in. She took a deep breath.

"There is someone who can stop the Baron. Bolt, the boy from the carriage. He saved me from hanging. Blazenda foretold he was the chosen one, although she was a little murky on what exactly he was chosen to do, but we're pretty sure he was chosen to fight the Baron and possibly save all of us. We need to help him." She took another deep breath and added, "He's my friend."

Her father grimaced. "A friend? Bandits don't have friends."

"I know," said Annika. "It just sort of happened." She sunk her head, mad at herself for allowing herself to care about someone other than a fellow bandit, although she had to admit that having a friend felt good.

"Annika is right," said Frau Farfenugen. "He is our only hope."

Vigi looked away, frowning, but when he lifted his head back up, the frown had turned into a small, wry smile. "Then we should find this boy." Annika looked at her father with uncertainty. She had seen that smile before, after he cheated at cards. She didn't trust that smile. Bandits never cheated at cards unless they were losing, but Vigi wasn't a very good card player, so he cheated often.

The group reversed course, heading back to town. They walked silently, like wind upon grass. Only Frau Farfenugen's clumsy and untrained-as-a-bandit footsteps, even louder because she wore combat boots, betrayed their movements.

"Can we visit my mother's grave on the way?" asked the housekeeper. "It's in the penguin cemetery."

"I'd like to see it," said Vigi. "But we'll hide while you visit and give you some privacy. Then we'll find the boy." He tossed an apple in the air. "If we run into any problems, I'm ready."

45.
The Bandit's Daughters

olt woke up. His head throbbed, his wrists hurt because they were tied tightly behind his back and to a tree, and his elbow itched but he couldn't scratch it, which was the most frustrating part of it all.

The storm had continued. Snow covered him like a firm white blanket and fell in huge flakes, each as big as a chestnut.

Bolt fought to free himself, but without success. He felt his face flush, and anger swirled inside him. He opened his mouth and let loose a loud . . .

BARK!

He clamped his mouth shut. His fury was the Baron's fury and he needed to force it out. The thought of the Baron angered him—how the monster had twisted the penguins' minds, how he had murdered Bolt's family. There was quite a lot to be angry about, actually. But anger was the enemy. Bolt could not let himself be like the Baron. He needed to calm himself.

"Nice barking," said a man's voice. "I must admit you not only look vaguely penguin-ish, but you sound like one, too."

Five giant penguins surrounded Bolt. At least they looked like penguins, the snow obscuring them, until Bolt realized that they were men in tattered clothing and penguin hats. He wiggled the flakes off his head, although more instantly replaced them.

They were in a large clearing, deep in the middle of the Brugarian forest, surrounded by dozens of tents. The place smelled like an old bathroom, despite the many air fresheners hanging from the trees. A scattering of fires kept the area warm, although not warm enough to melt the snow. It was late, and moon glow peeked out from behind a dark storm cloud but was quickly swallowed up again. In that brief instant, Bolt felt his skin tingling. It was not midnight yet, but the hour grew close.

As his vision continued to focus, Bolt more clearly made out the faces of the penguin bandits near him. Annika stood closest. Vigi Lambda stood by her side.

Annika turned to her father. "You have to release him."

Vigi shook his head. His lips curled into a horrible grin—big lips that seemed built for flute playing. In another life, perhaps he would have reached elite flutist heights. But here, he was merely a bandit in a crude penguin hat. "Can't do that. Sorry."

"Let me go," pleaded Bolt. "I haven't done anything to you! I need to save Brugaria. The Baron is evil!"

"He's the only one who can save us, Papa," pleaded Annika.

"He's just a kid," said Vigi, shaking his head. "I'd rather put my trust in the Baron than this boy."

"He's Brugaria's only chance," said Annika.

"No!" shouted Vigi. "The Baron won't be pleased his lowly housekeeper has left him to live with us. But if I return the boy to him, maybe we can avoid his wrath." Vigi sighed and looked at Bolt. "I appreciate your willingness to fight for Brugaria. It's very admirable. To show my gratitude, I will do anything you ask, except release you, spare your life, or be kind in any way."

"Will you and your crew perform a variety show with juggling, a magician, and hula dancing?"

"OK, we won't do that either."

"But we are to be married," hissed a deep, raspy, and familiar voice. Frau Farfenugen emerged from behind the group of penguin-capped bandits, holding hands with the Fish Man. The dim light of the moon, peeking through thick clouds, made her warts shine brighter, and made her look more elderly. The Fish Man wore his all-black attire and white sneakers. He stood as tall as Brutus.

"It isss true," said the Fish Man. "We are engaged."

Vigi smiled and clapped. "I have a new daughter and, soon, a new son? This is a very happy day. That is, it's a happy day for me." He looked at Bolt. "For you, this day sort of stinks."

"Brugarian tradition demands a father grant his daughter's requests on her engagement day," said Frau Farfenugen. "Even if that daughter is a lowly former housekeeper."

"I will not perform a variety show!" shouted the bandit.

"No. Free the boy. Annika is right. He is our only hope."

Vigi furrowed his brow and stared at Bolt, as if lost in thought.

"If you set me free, I will find the Baron," Bolt promised. "I can stab him with the tooth of a killer whale while we are both being transformed into werepenguins, and end his reign of terror-to-be."

Vigi's eyes continued to stare at Bolt. "You're kidding, right? That's the plan? Is that even possible?"

"I'm not sure," admitted Bolt. "But people aren't transformed into werepenguins every day, you know."

In the distance, penguins barked. A band of them wandered nearby. Bolt could feel their presence patrolling the woods.

"Guard the fish sticks!" exclaimed Vigi. Brutus marched off.

"Remember the young flutist who dared challenge the previous Vigi Lambda?" asked Annika. "No one believed he could win that fight. But he did. Fate works in mysterious ways, does it not? Aren't I proof of that—a kidnapped infant finding a loving home with a ruthless clan of bandits?" She held her father's hand. "Where is that brave soul who fought against the odds for what he believed in? Where is that man who knows that it's not enough to love your family—you must be willing to fight for them, too?"

As Annika spoke, Bolt's mind drifted and joined the barking penguins. They were the same group of penguin ruffians he had seen earlier rummaging through the bowling-ball bag. The group was larger now, but among them was the younger penguin, the one that had called Bolt "brother." Now its brain felt angrier. Harder. Bolt knew that feeling: the Baron's control had tightened.

"Let Bolt go, Papa!" pleaded Annika. She grabbed on to her father's leg. "If not for Frau Farfenugen, release him for me."

Felipe, who had been standing near them, also approached Vigi. He grabbed on to the bandit leader's other leg. "I agree with your daughters. The Baron can't be trusted. I bet he even cheats at cards, especially when he's losing."

Vigi's face turned red and he coughed. "Um, that's sort of allowed by the Code of the Bandit, you know."

Felipe narrowed his eyes. "Not that I would do that," he added.

Felipe gripped Vigi's leg harder. "Release the boy," he pleaded.

"Release Bolt!" begged Annika, squeezing her father's leg.

"Release him," agreed Frau Farfenugen, nudging Annika over so she could grab part of Vigi's leg, too.

"Releassse him," echoed the Fish Man, who tried to grab one of Vigi's legs, but there was no room left for him. He stood off to the side and sulked.

"Let go of my legs!" shouted Vigi Lambda, shaking Annika, Frau Farfenugen, and Felipe off. He stomped his foot twice, but whether it was with grim determination or because his legs had fallen asleep from being squeezed so hard, it was difficult to tell. "I will not free the boy, and that is final."

Again, Bolt heard the penguins approaching. In his mind Bolt saw them, clear as he could see his feet in front of him, or even more clearly, because his feet were mostly buried in snow.

Bolt closed his eyes. He reached inside himself, and sowed his thoughts deep inside the waddle's cloudy bird minds, hoping his commands would take root. He called to them:

We are family. Family looks out for each other. Help me.

The penguin barks grew louder, closer. The bandits murmured and exchanged worried glances.

"They're just penguins, boys," said Vigi, smiling, although his smile revealed a sliver of concern. "As long as we guard our fish sticks, we'll be fine."

"They sound vexed," said one of his bandits. "And I don't really like fish sticks all that much, anyway. Why don't we ever eat hot dogs?"

The penguins emerged from the trees, snarling.

"They look angry," said Annika.

"Very angry," agreed Frau Farfenugen. "You don't want to see penguins very angry."

The penguins rushed forward. Vigi and the bandits crouched, prepared to battle an onslaught of wet, blubbery power dashing toward them.

At that instant the winds seemed to pick up force and the snow fell in larger flakes, obscuring the scene in front of Bolt. Screams mingled with penguin yelps and, in between flakes, Bolt spied the flashing of knives, and maybe the glint of a bobby pin.

"The penguinsss have gone mad!" bellowed the Fish Man from nearby.

Bolt struggled against his ropes. Up above, the moon was invisible behind the clouds, but Bolt's blood tingled. Midnight was so close!

A hand brushed against Bolt's. He felt his ropes untwisting.

"Will you save Brugaria?" asked Annika, slicing the rope around Bolt's wrists.

"I'll try," said Bolt. He stood up, rubbing his sore, rope-burned wrists.

Annika clutched his hands. For a moment Bolt forgot he had ever been an unwanted boy. For a moment he thought only one thing:

I have a friend. I am the chosen one. Also, I'm really hungry.

Or rather, he thought three things.

Annika released Bolt's hands and pointed to her left. "That is the way back to the manor. Maybe you'll find the Baron there. And thank you."

"For what?"

"For helping me understand that my place is here, with my family." She leaned over and gave him a quick hug. "Find the Baron. And save us all."

All around them, the penguin-bandit battle raged. They rolled and fought, bit and stabbed in the falling snow. Vigi screamed to his men, "Don't give up!" and "Protect the fish sticks!" Annika ran to join the battle.

The young penguin, Bolt's brother, emerged from the white. The bird stared at Bolt, its mind racing with feelings of viciousness but also of family, and of peace. Its eyes rolled around and then blinked over and over again. Apparently, small bird brains were not adept at thinking lots of different thoughts at once.

"Let me go," said Bolt. "We are brothers."

The penguin bowed, turned, and rushed back to join the fight. Bolt could not see who was winning and who was losing in the battle, not through the thick, falling snow.

The deafening sounds of barking and fighting echoed through the wintry night. Bolt dared not look back. The sounds grew fainter as he ran.

Midnight loomed.

46.
Fire and Ice

Bolt hurried through the forest in the direction Annika had pointed, or hurried as best he could. He kept turning to avoid trees, and then was unsure if he was still heading in the right direction or some other, random one. Meanwhile, the forest grew blacker. If total darkness could become even more total in its darkness, then that's what it did.

As Bolt ran, night-tearing flashes of lightning momentarily lit the way, but only for a blink of the eye.

The crisscrossing lightning cracked, a deafening boom followed, and a tree branch fell a few feet to Bolt's left, flames crackling. Another flash followed and a tree split in half to Bolt's right.

Lightning exploded in all directions, as if it wanted

him—a bolt for Bolt. *Pop. Crackle. Snap.* It was like running in a bowl of cereal.

Because of the fires, Bolt could now see his way, but he preferred the previous blackness to the fiery terror around him. Ashes blew. Heat scorched.

Finally, through the flickering flashes, the flaming branches, and the thunder-booming dark, Bolt reached the end of the forest. He stepped out of the woods and onto the Baron's lawn. The manor was unlit, covered by a gloominess that seemed to swallow the darkness around it.

As he ran, any remaining fragments of uncertainty withered away like old lettuce. He didn't even feel a flicker of temptation to run away.

Bolt was stronger now. He would never bolt from trouble again.

Bolt ran toward the manor. Above, snow tumbled down and, way above that, the moon, hidden behind clouds, snuck out. Bolt felt the skin on his arms tingle, and his hairs rise up.

Then the moon resumed its hiding place and, just as suddenly as it had started, the tingling ceased.

From the yard, Bolt heard the grandfather clock chime, on and on and on. Twelve times. When it finished, Bolt had not transformed.

He was still human. Had the curse somehow been lifted?

He remembered the Fortune Teller's final words to

him. She'd said they didn't mean much. But they meant everything.

"The curse comes from the moon. You can only transform when it shines."

The moon changed Bolt. While the clouds covered its glow, Bolt's transformation was delayed.

And so must be the Baron's.

Bolt needed to stab the Baron while they were both turning into werepenguins. Bolt had a chance, if only the clouds would stay still.

He ran faster, sprinting across the manor lawn. He reached the house and slammed open the door, thankful it wasn't locked. Maybe luck was on his side. If he got lucky, he would find the Baron waiting. If he got really, really lucky, he'd find the Baron and stab him before they completed their penguin transformations. "Baron? Where are you? Come out!" There was no answer.

Apparently, this was not his lucky day after all. The Baron was not home.

Shouting from outside jarred Bolt's disappointment. He dashed to the window, peeled back the curtain, and peered out. A line of people marched toward the house holding torches. They all wore fuzzy blue robes.

They shouted: "We'll get you! . . . You're surrounded! . . . I can't believe I postponed my vacation for this!"

It was the Mystical Brotherhood, or Sisterhood, or something else of Whales, united.

At their head stood Günter. He wagged his French bread. Franz stood by his side.

"Come out, Baron!" screamed the whale prince. The horde behind him clapped and cheered and raised their flames high.

"We've got torches!" yelled Franz.

"And I've got my French bread!" yelled Günter.

"Yes, but torches are better," said Franz.

"Bread!"

"Torches!"

"Bread!"

"How about if you hit the Baron with your bread and then we use our torches?" suggested Franz.

Günter shrugged. "I can live with that."

Bolt shrank back into the shadows of the house, wondering if he could sneak out and escape. He needed to find the Baron. He couldn't linger here, wasting time fighting the outside throng.

"The house is surrounded. You have no choice but to surrender," yelled Günter. On the lawn, he was bathed in light. The moon had peeked out from the clouds.

Bolt's nose twitched and expanded, growing rapidly. He kicked off his shoes, as his feet grew larger and orange. It was too late. He had lost, and was doomed to be a penguin for eternity.

Or was he? The tingling stopped. His nose stopped expanding. He wasn't changing. Not anymore, anyway.

Through the window, Bolt saw the clouds hovering over the moon, blocking it from view. The glow around the Prince of Whales had ceased.

"The Baron's not here!" Bolt shouted out the open door.

"It's the Baron's boy. The whale hater!" shouted Günter, waving his bread loaf high in the air. "Or something boy-ish," he added, squinting at Bolt's part-penguin head.

"Leave me alone!" Bolt cried. "We are on the same side. I need to fight the Baron. I can stop him. And honestly, I don't hate whales."

"Do you think we were born yesterday?" demanded Günter.

"I was born on a Saturday," said Franz.

A window shattered and a large loaf of French bread landed near Bolt's feet.

"Take that!" yelled Günter from outside. After a pause he yelled, "Anyone have more French bread I can borrow?"

"Let's smoke him out!" cried Franz.

A few members of the Brotherhood, or Sisterhood, or whatever, hurled their torches at the manor. Flames licked the manor's walls. The winds howled and lightning crashed again, searing part of the manor.

Smoke blew into the house through the broken glass. Bolt choked on its fumes. He needed to reach higher ground, away from the smoldering walls and the billow-ing black soot.

He scaled the staircase steps, two at a time, up to the landing, and then up and up and around and around again to the top of the tower. The smoke chased him, spreading up the stairwell after him, only inches behind him. Flames quickly engulfed the lower floors. Bolt couldn't go back down even if he wanted to.

Bolt reached the top of the stairs and burst into his room as smoke streamed in from the secret tunnel entrance. Down below, on the lawn, the townspeople shouted, their voices rising up with the air-choking smoke. Out the window, flames scaled the walls. The fire was spreading fast, surprisingly so, as if the house were made from paper. It wasn't, of course. It was made of wood and penguin blubber, but penguin blubber burns quickly.

Bolt couldn't give up. Not now, not with so many depending on him. Villagers! Penguins! Annika! Maybe even warty children-to-be!

Bolt closed his eyes, and he could sense the penguins, hundreds huddled together on the Blacker Sea shore. Although they gathered far away, Bolt could now feel the birds' thoughts, muddled and frightened and filled with the Baron's ruthless commands.

That was where Bolt would find the Baron.

He flung open the window, took a deep breath, and leapt.

Penguins were good jumpers. The moon had changed

Bolt already, somewhat. He hoped it had changed him enough. If not, his life would end now, splattered onto the ground below.

THUMP! His feet landed at the edge of the roof. Then they slipped back, slipping, slipping, and slipping down, down, down the slanted shingles, many broken and crumbling. Bolt dug his webbed feet into the roof to get a grip. But his feet slipped, not gripped.

The clouds parted for a brief moment, a split second really, but in that moment, the moon's rays shone and Bolt's feet grew an inch, maybe less, but just enough to stick onto the roof's shingles a tad more.

Bolt stopped sliding with half of his webbed foot dangling over the side of the roof.

He scrambled up toward the catapult, where the roof flattened.

The faraway shore lit up from the lightning strikes. The waves whipped against the rocks. Meanwhile, the flames danced over the side of the house and rose into the sky, carrying cinders up against the falling snow.

Once more, a cloud shifted. One of his arms became a small wing. His stomach expanded, ripping through his shirt, and a big blubbery white mass protruded over his pants. And then, again, the transformation stopped as the moon disappeared behind a cloud.

Every time the moon peeked out, Bolt grew closer to penguin-hood and an eternal curse, while Brugaria and the penguins and bandits all grew closer to doom. Much of Bolt had changed, but his mind was still his. That would be the last to transform.

"He's trapped!" cried Günter from the lawn below. The Brotherhood, or Sisterhood, or whatever they were called, had spotted Bolt on the roof. The whale folk shouted in celebration. They raised their torches and exchanged high fives. They thought all was lost for Bolt, and that he had no way to escape.

They were wrong.

Bolt had never fired a catapult before. It wasn't something he'd thought he would ever need to do, but it didn't seem difficult. He stepped into the basket connected to the end of the throwing arm, a basket large enough for boulders, just wide enough for Bolt.

As the villagers shouted in alarm, realizing what was about to happen, a blast of lightning struck the side of the manor from the violent thunder snowstorm. Bolt slashed his teeth, now penguin sharp, against the tether. The catapult rocketed up and flung Bolt out into the sky and toward the shore.

47.
The Battle along the Blacker Sea

It was peaceful up here, amid the snow and wind. In the air, high above the lawn and the forest, the thunder silenced and the lightning halted. Bolt heard nothing.

This was how a bird felt. Not a penguin, since they were flightless, but geese and doves and eagles and other winged creatures.

Bolt hated it. His kind was not meant to fly, but to be earth- and water-bound. He did not belong up here near the trembling clouds and the ghastly mix of black and faint violet lights that reminded Bolt of a purple pen running out of ink.

Bolt soared over the trees and toward the shoreline. He could see all of Volgelplatz from up here: the village

to the shore. Ahead, a large cluster of penguins waddled in the shallow water. And where Bolt found penguins, he would find the Baron.

He sailed past the final line of trees, the sandy beach growing closer. Bolt thrust his half-penguin body forward as he landed on his penguin-turned stomach.

OOMPH!

Bolt smashed into the ground, but instead of plopping heavily, his belly slid like a well-oiled eel on the wet, snow-covered sand.

He skidded to a stop just a few feet from the rocking waves crashing against the Blacker Sea's shore. As soon as his skidding ceased, the thunder growled and the lightning resumed its display.

Hundreds of penguins stood around Bolt, staring at him. Afraid. Bolt sensed it. He held out his hand. He opened his mind. The Baron was not here. Not yet. But he was coming, of that Bolt was certain.

I won't hurt you. Bolt fought against his own anger, concentrating on sending words of hopefulness across the beach. *I'm here to help. I'm your brother.* He tried to connect with each of the birds, spreading his message into the air, where it nestled inside the penguin brains, soothing them and showing the birds there was another way, a better way. A family way.

As if on cue, the thunder grew softer and the crackling tentacles of electricity shifted away from the beach.

The storm was passing, although the clouds still blocked the moon.

Bolt filled his mind—and the penguins' minds—with thoughts of smiling chicks and loving parents. He thought of festive picnics, vacation road trips, and games of water polo, and then removed the water polo thoughts since he decided that wasn't something most families really did together. But he let his imagination soar, filling the air with pure, unbridled emotion: joy and love and celebration and fish sticks. He wished he hadn't thought of fish sticks, but he was very hungry.

Unlike the Baron's malicious thoughts, Bolt's spoke a sort of penguin truth: we are peaceful, family-loving birds.

Turning their thoughts was easy. *This* was what Bolt was chosen to do.

But there were so many penguins—hundreds if not thousands. Bolt wasn't sure if all of them heard his message. The Baron had clouded the birds' brains for so long.

Unite. Family. Love.

He could hear a few of their minds answering back.

We are family . . . We will protect each other . . .

The penguins stood in place, emitting loud braying calls and bobbing to the right and left. Bolt continued spreading his message. *We are family!* More penguins echoed his thoughts, some as a question, but others as a statement.

We are family?

Yes, we are family!

The more Bolt hammered his message, the more the gray clouds of the Baron's evil thoughts dispersed. *Families take care of each other.* The penguins wobbled in agreement. *You can be a family again. All of you. If only we stand up to the Baron. Together.*

An enormous splash filled the sea behind them, and Bolt turned to see a large flipper sailing up from the watery depths. A spray of water shot into the sky and a set of teeth—the largest Bolt had ever seen—seemed to swallow the world.

The orca. It was here, with all its devastating might. Mostly black, but with a white underbelly, the killer whale leapt out of the sea in a tight arc. Lightning ripped apart the sky, its glare reflecting off the whale's long and powerful choppers. Water sprayed from the mammal's blowhole.

Whatever comfort Bolt had tried to provide for the penguins a moment earlier vanished. Frightened, the birds ran from the shore. Their thoughts of family were ripped away and replaced with the primal urge for survival. Bolt wanted to run, too, but he fought the impulse. He needed to be calm. *Don't be afraid . . . You are safe . . .*

Some answered back.

We are with you . . . We understand . . . But help, it's a whale!

Other noises erupted from the woods opposite the water. Countless penguins waddled out from one side of the forest, and they brought a barking wall of anger. The fleeing penguins halted. The barking penguins hissed.

Bolt hadn't heard this new group coming; his mind had been too busy reaching out to the penguins at the beach, trying to comfort them, and also trying to calm himself and to stop thinking of fish sticks so much. But now there were more penguins than he could count, and a steel door of anger surrounded their brains.

The Baron strode out of the forest, his mind spreading across the beach like the shadow from a blimp. He too had half changed from the cloud-hidden moon. His face was that of a penguin but he had the body of a boy, still dressed in his black pants, tuxedo shirt, and cape, although his webbed feet had ripped through his shoes, leaving only a few strands of leather attached to the soles.

Bolt reached for his whale-tooth necklace with his one non-wing hand. If Blazenda was right, it was the only way to put an end to the Baron's immortality, and also break his own curse. Bolt ripped the tooth from its chain and gripped it tightly.

"Going somewhere?" snapped the Baron, his voice a high, half-penguin squeak.

"Just visiting family," said Bolt. "My family." He continued thinking happy thoughts. More and more penguins were responding to his hopeful message of togetherness.

But a storm of rage flowed from the Baron. Bolt's happier thoughts pushed against the Baron's menace. It was an invisible war, one evenly matched for now, yet one Bolt knew he would lose once the clouds moved again. After the moon lit the beach, Bolt would become a werepenguin forever and all would be lost.

But that time had not yet come.

We are family!

The Baron-penguin growled at Bolt. "All I wanted was for us to be BFFs: Bird Friends Forever. Was that too much to ask?"

"You didn't want a BFF. You wanted a slave."

"Same difference," said the Baron.

"No. BFFs care for each other. Respect each other. Just like family does."

"You sound like a greeting card," hissed the Baron.

"Really? I've never gotten a greeting card," admitted Bolt.

"Join me and you can have all the greeting cards you want. I'll give you one more chance. I'm willing to forget this. You'll get used to being a despised creature of the midnight moon. Trust me. Sure, the manor is in flames. Yes, I need to buy some new tuxedos because we keep ripping through ours every time we transform into penguins. But you and I are kings, Humboldt. The true Penguin Kings. These penguins know we are their leaders."

"No!" cried Bolt. "You killed my parents. I'll never follow you! Besides, the penguins don't need a leader. They need a family. I'm not their ruler. I'm their brother." He sensed the Baron's thoughts creeping into his own, and he shook his head. The invisible thought war raged all around them.

Hurt! Attack!

No, we are family!

"You can't control me," said Bolt.

"Not yet, it seems. But those clouds won't hide the moon forever. Face it. You're a natural, Humboldt. Look how you speak to the penguins. See how they listen to you. Just think of it! When these penguins salute me, someday, I'll make sure they salute you, too."

"I heard penguins never salute."

"They will," the Baron snarled. "And then we will take our rightful place as the rulers of all Brugaria. With the penguin army obeying our every command, the world will soon bow to us."

"And what of the people?"

"The commoners? Who cares? Some will be dinner. Others will languish in dungeons. Those who are lucky will work in the fish stick kitchens or labor deep in the salt mines."

"We have salt mines?"

"Not yet, but that's because we don't have laborers. Anyway, this is your last chance, Humboldt. Join me!"

Bolt pictured Annika frying large fish under the tyranny of an evil penguin foreman. He saw the villagers shackled in cells. He even imagined the housekeeper, Frau

Farfenugen, being chewed by hungry penguins—but he didn't imagine it for more than a moment because it was too gruesome. "Never!"

"Very well." The Baron pointed to Bolt. "Penguins, attack! Show him the power of our wrath!"

The penguins did not move.

"Don't you hear me?" cried the Baron.

Still the penguins remained where they stood.

"They hear you," said Bolt. "But they are done obeying. Penguins are about family. About protecting each other. They now know there's another way."

The penguins barked and Bolt understood them perfectly. *We are family!*

The Baron's face turned purple with fury, and then blue, and then back to purple. He trembled. "They will listen to me once you are defeated. But now I am very angry. And as I have warned, you do not want to see me very angry!"

The Family That Fights Together

Before Bolt faced the Baron, before he even reached the manor, while he was running through the dark forest with trees blazing in lightning-blasted flames and the snow coming down in acorn-size flakes, Annika and the bandits were fighting the penguins that had helped Bolt escape.

Brutus, the largest bandit, threw a piano at them, but it didn't help very much. All he did was ruin an expensive piano.

Felipe had fought, but he'd left his knife in his tent, so all he had were toenail clippings and postage stamps, both of which were as useless as a piano in a fight.

But the bandits had other weapons. Vigi hurled apples with skillful aim. Annika ducked and dove out of the way of flapping wings, distracting the penguins with her nimble speed while other bandits hit birds on the head with sticks and stones. A few bandits had small crusty pieces of French bread left over from dinner, which proved to be effective weapons.

Once Bolt had flown the coop, so to speak, the penguins quickly lost their desire to fight. They ran away, although not without swiping a box of fish sticks from the bandits' fish stick tent.

Most of the bandits, breathing heavily, lay down to catch their breaths. Other than random nicks and bruises, no bandits were injured, and only a couple needed bandages.

Vigi's eyes rested on the ropes that had bound Bolt but now lay on the ground. He scowled and cursed to himself. His eyes rested on Annika. "You released him, didn't you?"

Annika nodded. "I'm sorry, Papa. But he can save us. He can save all of Brugaria."

"We're bandits! What do we care of Brugaria?" Vigi demanded.

"We are not just bandits, but Brugarian Forest Bandits," Annika reminded him. "We need all of the Brugarians free, so that we can kidnap and rob them. In a way, they are our family, too."

"A family we kidnap and rob," said Vigi.

"Exactly," said Annika.

"She is right, Daddy," said Frau Farfenugen. She had not fought the penguins; she had no bandit training. Instead, she and the Fish Man had hidden behind a tree. But when the fighting ceased, they joined the rest of the group. "My entire life I have been nothing but a lowly housekeeper, worrying about myself and hoping the Baron would not get very angry and eat me, or tape me to the wall and play Pin the Tail on the Donkey, with me as the donkey. But now that I am free, I know this isn't just about me, or my fear of donkey tails. I am also a Brugarian. We must help Bolt, band together, and defeat the Baron."

Vigi pulled at his hair. He gritted his teeth. "I know you're right, but I have to protect you, and all the bandits!" He curled his hands into fists and pounded his legs in frustration. Then he winced, because he'd pounded his legs too hard. "What should I do? There aren't rules in the Code of the Bandit on how to raise a family. Right, Felipe?"

Felipe, who had been standing to the side, looked down at his feet. "Actually I've never read the code. It's way too long and boring. Sorry." Vigi stared at Felipe, stunned.

Felipe looked back up. "But I don't have to read a bandit code to know that not all things need to be written down to be true. You must be ready to fight for the things you love. We need to fight for each other."

"I might not know everything about being a bandit," admitted Annika. "Not yet, anyway. But even I know that."

Vigi wrapped his arms around Annika. His eyes watered. "What did I do to deserve such a wonderful daughter?"

"You kidnapped me?" Annika guessed, but her eyes watered, too.

Tears rolled down Vigi's cheeks now, and he didn't care that bandits weren't supposed to cry unless they were about to be hanged. He would need to revise that part of the code.

"Can we find Bolt and fight with him now?" asked Annika.

"Of course," said Vigi. He embraced Annika and added, "You'll make a wonderful bandit someday."

"I know," said Annika, returning her father's hug.

49.
The Return of the Whale

Back at the beach, the Baron was very, very, very angry.

The air around him seemed to ripple, and the foamy mist from the Blacker Sea popped like squeezed blemishes.

The Baron's penguin head vibrated from side to side, faster and faster, until his features blurred, and then it did three complete turns on his neck.

When his head stopped spinning, steam erupted from his ears.

The Baron's beak grew and enlarged by four inches. From his mouth, razor-sharp twin fangs sprouted.

His tuxedo shredded into pieces as the Baron grew larger, taller, wider. He now stood a foot taller than Bolt, his eyes blazed red, and his beak twisted into a diabolical sneer.

The Baron-penguin monster opened his mouth, and the loudest bark Bolt had ever heard rang out, so loud that Bolt would not have been surprised if the orphans all the way back at Oak Wilt could hear it.

But even more horrifying were the new, even darker evil thoughts erupting from the Baron-penguin's mind like an angry volcano, spreading a cloud of hate and violence through the shoreline with such force that Bolt staggered back.

The Baron-penguin plodded forward. Bolt held the tooth by his side like a dagger. He dug his webbed feet into the snow.

The moon peeked out from behind a cloud, and Bolt felt his ears shrink and the webbing on his feet expand. His mind grew dizzy. He couldn't concentrate. He was going to lose his chance. All was lost.

But then the moon ducked behind a cloud, and Bolt's brain snapped back awake. Bolt clenched the daggerlike tooth tighter. He had to stab the Baron now, before the moon danced out again. Even one more moon peek might be too much for Bolt to overcome.

The Baron-penguin flung himself at Bolt, who lifted the tooth up. But Bolt hadn't expected the partly transformed Baron to be so fast, or so powerful. The creature rammed into Bolt before the tooth was in position.

Bolt fell back onto the sand. The Baron-penguin stood next to him, and slapped Bolt's head with a wing.

"You don't have a chance," snarled the beast, slapping Bolt again and again. "I'm stronger than you." He smiled and flashed his terrible fangs. "You will make a wonderful dinner." A drop of saliva dripped onto Bolt's eye.

"Gross," said Bolt.

Lightning lit up the sea. The killer whale gnashed its teeth within the rolling, crashing waves. The penguins on the beach squawked with fear, their fright slicing through the dark thoughts emanating from the Baron-penguin.

Distracted, the Baron-penguin looked back at the mighty orca.

Bolt rolled out from under his enemy and scrambled to his webbed feet.

A loud shout blared from the woods and then the entire Mystical Brotherhood, or Sisterhood, or whatever they were called, emerged from the forest, Günter and Franz in the lead. One side of the tree line was filled with penguins, and the opposite side was filled with torch-waving whale lovers.

The penguins stared at them, some with evil snarls but others smiling, their thoughts free of the Baron's hate-filled cloud, their minds singing, *We are family.*

The songs stirred within Bolt. The chants grew inside him, fueling him with hope and determination.

More sounds blared from the forest, and the Brugarian

Forest Bandits emerged, led by Annika and Vigi Lambda.

"We're here to help!" shouted Annika.

"I was wrong," called Vigi Lambda. "Annika's wisdom has convinced me. We will stand with you against the Baron." He held an apple. "I'm even ready to waltz, if needed."

The Baron-penguin hissed at Vigi Lambda. "You and the bandits will pay dearly for this. Once I dispose of the boy, you are next. You will cry for mercy."

Vigi Lambda raised his chin. "Actually, crying is strictly prohibited by the Code of the Bandit, although I am planning on changing that part."

Then another shout rang out from the woods, and another group emerged, men, women, and children, one hundred people deep. The witch hat and black wedding dress–clad Fortune Teller, Blazenda, led them. "We shall protect Brugaria!" she shouted, and then cackled. "Sorry about the cackling, it is a bad habit but not really appropriate right now."

"Get him!" yelled one of the villagers behind Blazenda, pointing to the Baron-penguin.

"No! Stand back!" ordered Blazenda. "The boy has to be the one to do it."

The villagers hesitated, staying close to the tree line, as did the others.

The Baron-penguin spat on the ground.

Bolt lunged toward him, tooth in hand. The tooth's sharp point neared the creature's penguin hide.

But the beast was not so easily defeated. He leapt aside and at the same time back-swatted Bolt with a powerful wing. Bolt landed on the sandy ground, dazed. His hand hit a rock, and the tooth slipped from his grip.

Bolt was toothless.

The world spun. Bolt scanned the ground around him, but his vision was blurry and unfocused. Where was the tooth?

There it was, by the edge of the shore, just a few feet away. He crawled onto his side and reached out his arm.

A wave rolled in from the sea and when it ebbed, the tooth was gone.

Bolt screamed and jumped up, ready to dive into the water to find his weapon, when a wing slapped his head. The Baron-penguin stood once more above the fallen Bolt, his beak curved into a hideous smile.

"Face it, Humboldt. You will never defeat me." He raised his wing, ready to crash it down on Bolt's head. Bolt winced, picturing a hammer smashing into a watermelon, with Bolt's head as the watermelon.

The wing never lowered. A small penguin rammed into the Baron-penguin's legs, and the Baron toppled over. It was Bolt's penguin brother, whom Bolt had embraced earlier and seen again at the bandit camp. He stood on top of the Baron's stomach, jumping up and down.

The penguin barked. *Family! Family!*

Growling, the Baron-penguin flicked the penguin

away as if he were nothing more than a troublesome guppy. Bolt's brother flew to the ground and landed on the sand with a loud thud.

A small rock bounced off the Baron-penguin's head. Then another rock, and then what looked like a bobby pin hit him in the eye. The monster blinked, but did not appear to be injured, or even mildly inconvenienced.

"Go, Bolt! Get the tooth! I'll distract him!" Annika urged, hurling more rocks at the Baron.

Bolt staggered to his feet and ran toward the Blacker Sea. He dove into the foamy waves, his eyes searching the bottom, but could see nothing but sand and rocks.

A moment later he heard the Baron leap into the water behind him.

Up ahead, in the sea, the killer whale jumped and splashed—nine tons of ferocious, penguin-eating hunger. The surface exploded from its weight. Bolt could have sworn he saw the orca lick its teeth when it realized Bolt was swimming in its direction.

But Bolt needed that tooth. Where was it?

Fear erupted inside Bolt's head as he kept his head above water, gasping for air. His penguin instincts were warning him to turn away from the whale. The orca was his natural enemy. But those same instincts shouted, *We are family!* Bolt kicked faster. His webbed feet motored him forward. The tooth was at the bottom of the sea. Bolt dove, a wing and an arm outstretched to grab the weapon.

Bolt was a thunderbolt. Fierce. Unstoppable.

The Baron grabbed one of Bolt's legs as Bolt's fingertips grazed the tooth. Bolt kicked to free himself. He rolled under the waves, but the Baron-penguin wouldn't let go. Bolt rolled three more times, but the monster's grasp was too firm. Bolt lashed out with a wing, slapping the beast alongside the head, but the Baron-penguin merely laughed. The waves silenced the sounds, but Bolt saw the monster's mad and gloating grin. The tide took them farther out to sea as they jabbed and slapped, rolled and kicked, in and above the waves. The tooth was behind them, somewhere.

The killer whale neared them, watching. Bolt ignored the near-paralyzing fear that coursed through him. If the Baron shared that fear, he did not show it. Bolt had been bobbing above the surface, but the Baron grabbed Bolt's hair and forced his face back under the water.

Bolt didn't have a penguin head yet, just the start of a beak. He couldn't hold his breath as long as a completely transformed werepenguin could. He thrashed with all his might.

The Baron adjusted his grip, and Bolt lifted his head from the water and breathed the welcome air. The misty sea salt splashed down his throat, and he choked.

"You don't have a chance," the Baron growled. "You aren't nearly as strong as I am. I have one hundred years of penguin-ism. Prepare to meet your end. We are *not*

family. I will make the bandits and the villagers and the penguins all suffer for your insolence."

Behind the Baron, the sea erupted.

The orca rose out of the depths, its mouth stretched open. Bolt kicked the Baron-penguin with his webbed feet, forcing himself away from the whale while putting his enemy directly into its path. The orca chomped its killer whale teeth down. The Baron howled, but it was too late.

The whale swallowed the Baron in one gulp.

The enormous mammal released a happy burp before diving under the water and disappearing into the sea.

From the shore, the villagers cheered, raising their torches. Members of the whale Brotherhood, or Sisterhood, or something else–hood, hugged bandits, and bandits hugged penguins. Günter hugged Franz.

Bolt let his mind drift over the shore. The heavy cloud of hate from the Baron was dissipating, but it was Bolt's calm and loving thoughts that soothed the penguins. Soon, all the penguins barked, *"We are family!"*

It would take time, but soon every penguin mind would be restored back to its innocent, peaceful nature.

The penguins, every last one of them, looked at Bolt as he swam in from the sea. Raising his head from the waves, he could see them. They raised their wings. For a moment, they looked like the statues in the graveyard. They saluted Bolt.

He couldn't imagine feeling more part of a family than he felt at that moment.

Bolt had everything he ever wanted.

The waves pulled Bolt back to shore. As his webbed feet touched the sandy shoreline, Annika ran up to him. "Are you OK? I mean, other than being a half-penguin monster?"

Bolt looked down at his wing, his penguin stomach, and his webbed feet. "I guess so."

"Stop him!" yelled Günter, running toward Bolt with

Franz by his side. "The boy is a menace!" He held a new, extra-crispy loaf of French bread over his head.

Other whale folk ran behind him, as did some villagers. A few raised pitchforks. Others held shovels. "Stop the whale hater!" the people cried.

"I really don't hate the whales, although that orca was pretty frightening," said Bolt, cringing. He had no desire to fight all these villagers, and doubted he could anyway, not alone. Had he beat the Baron only to meet his end here, on the beach?

Maybe he could still bolt.

But before he turned to flee, Annika jumped in front of him. "Leave Bolt alone. He just saved all of us."

"He's a monster," insisted Günter. "Get out of my way."

The other villagers yelled, too. "Get him! He's a monster!"

Vigi Lambda ran up next to his daughter and rubbed his fingers along a crisp red apple. "You'll have to go through me, too."

"And me." A scratchy ancient voice cackled through the other sounds, along with what sounded like wind chimes playing the Alphabet Song. It was Blazenda, and she locked arms with Vigi and Annika. "This boy is the chosen hero." She turned her head to Bolt. "But I have to admit, I thought you were chosen to be slaughtered by the Baron."

"He is a hero," agreed Annika. "Thanks to Bolt, Baron

Chordata is no more." Although she spoke his name, no one screamed or fainted. The mood lightened. Villagers nodded their heads. Pitchforks were lowered. Shovels were dropped to the ground.

Even Günter put down his French bread. "Well, maybe he doesn't hate whales all that much."

"Come live with us. We can be like brother and sister," said Annika, taking Bolt's non-wing hand in hers.

"We'll look past your flippers," said Vigi. "I've already added a warty, greenish daughter today, why not a penguin-ish son, too?"

Bolt looked into Annika's eyes. It was tempting. A sister. A family. Maybe even a real family.

"I know we're bandits and we live in a forest," said Annika. "Which isn't always very comfortable. But nothing is more important than family."

"Even kidnapping and carriage robbing are less important, although only a little less," added Vigi Lambda.

"They are right," said Günter. "Family is everything. I had a daughter once. She vanished one night. I always assumed she was kidnapped, but I never got a ransom note."

"Wait," said Vigi. "Is your address 919?"

"No, it's 616, why?"

"No reason," said Vigi, coughing and looking away.

Annika put her arm around Bolt. "See, Bolt? You told me once that you would always be unwanted. But I want you. My father wants you. All of Volgelplatz wants you.

You taught me there is nothing more important than family. A family can be a mom or a dad or a grandparent. But it can also be a group of bandits or a village."

Bolt felt his skin tremble as the moon finally peeked out from behind a cloud. His small penguin friend stood by the side, wing to wing with the other penguins. It barked.

Brother?

Above, the clouds slowly drifted away from the moon. "Thank you, but I have a family already," Bolt said to Annika. "And they are waiting for someone to help them find their way. My brothers and sisters need me. We are family."

The storm clouds lifted. Light from the pure, unfiltered, always-full Brugarian moon beamed down over the water and onto Bolt. Bolt dashed beneath the water, and the penguins, thousands of them, ran after him and joined him in the sea.

EPILOGUE

Midnight at the St. Aves Zoo

The man stopped talking. It took me a moment to remember where I was, here at the St. Aves Zoo. My watch showed it was a minute before midnight. The time had gone quickly.

I sneezed again and reached for my tissues. I wiped my nose. There was only one tissue left.

"What happened next?" I asked.

"That's the end of the story."

"The end?" I shrieked. "How can it be the end? What about 'Happily ever after' or 'And then Bolt turned back into a human'? There are a million ways to end a story, but yours was not one of them."

"Make-believe tales may end, but life does not. It just goes on."

"What happened to Bolt?"

"He found the family he always wanted. He was loved, and he loved back, and that's really the most important thing."

"Was Bolt ever adopted?"

The man shrugged.

"Was his curse lifted?" I persisted.

The man shrugged again.

"There's a lot of shrugging going on," I pointed out.

The man shrugged one more time.

"What of the girl? Annika?"

"No one knows for certain what happened to her. But I've heard tell of a Brugarian bandit, a woman, although she goes by the name Vigi Lambda. Many say she is the greatest bandit who ever lived." The man smiled, a smile of longing, but not of regret. Whatever choices he had made in life, he was content with them. "Should I have the penguins ready for you, when you depart in the morning?"

I frowned. I scowled. My shoulders sagged. "No. I cannot take your penguins. My employers will be disappointed, but how can I break up a family, or remove them from such a comfortable home? Your story, it seems, has done its job, my friend, even if it means I can no longer do mine. But still, I thank you."

"For what?"

"For opening my eyes. I've always thought of a zoo as merely a cage for animals, for them to be gaped at for the public's amusement. But perhaps animals deserve a happy home and a family, too. I have a lot to think about."

The man bowed. "I am glad my story could enlighten you. Now, it is only a few seconds before midnight and I must take my leave. When midnight strikes, my work here is just beginning."

I sneezed not once, but twice. I used the very last tissue. By the time I looked back up, the man had neared the penguin exhibit. He waddled the entire way.

"In the end, Bolt was wanted," the man said, looking back at me as he opened the exhibit door. "He loved his home. He found a family. He couldn't have asked for a better life."

He walked through the door and as he did, his jacket rode up his back. I could have sworn it revealed a black penguin tail just starting to grow.

"What are you doing here?" A guard, burly and strong, grabbed my arm. "It's midnight. The zoo closed hours ago. You need to leave, sir."

"The man I was talking to just now," I said, as the guard led me away. "What was his name? The penguin caretaker."

"There's no penguin caretaker here," huffed the guard. "You're imagining things."

I looked back to the exhibit one last time. Fifteen pen-guins barked at me.

Although I could have sworn there had only been four-teen penguins just a moment before.

TURN THE PAGE TO
BEGIN READING . . .

THE REVENGE OF THE
WEREPENGUIN

1.
My Life as a Penguin

It was a city of snow: the glaciers were its skyscrapers, the floating ice sheets its roads, and the thousands of penguins barking along the seashore its remarkably well-dressed, tuxedo-clad citizens.

Humboldt Wattle—people had called him Bolt back when there were other people around to call him anything—was almost thirteen but not quite, and he was a penguin, but also not quite and certainly not at that very moment. He sat in the snow on a hill wearing only a pair of ripped sweatpants and a thin, tattered T-shirt. That outfit would have been quite insufficient to keep anyone else comfortable in this frozen tundra, but Bolt was cozy. He couldn't feel cold.

Bolt *could*, however, feel the thoughts of his penguin

brothers and sisters waddling along the shore, although he was not one of them. Not truly. He would never lay an egg, or at least he hoped he wouldn't. He would never molt. He would never spend his afternoon frolicking in the arctic sea.

He would only frolic in the arctic sea at night.

For such was Bolt's plight, to turn into a penguin under a full moon. But those nights! They were glorious! He would swim with his family, yowl with them, and carouse with them.

It was too bad full moons were so few and far between. The rest of the time, Bolt was merely human, or at least mostly so. For despite his outside appearance, Bolt had penguin blood surging inside him. He could read penguin minds. He could talk with them, play with them, and love them. Always.

But. There was a something deep down inside the birds, a barrier that was hard and round and slightly crusty, and no matter how hard Bolt tried to be penetrate that crust, he couldn't quite do it. That crusty something was primal and ancient and alien to Bolt, and it separated him from the rest of the rookery. Before joining this colony, before even coming to Brugaria, Bolt had been an unwanted orphan. It seemed that, no matter what he did and how far he traveled, he would never truly feel wanted, not completely, on land or in sea.

For that was his curse: the curse of the werepenguin.

As Bolt sat on his snowy hill, he rubbed his fingers against a slim gold chain around his neck. That chain had once held a killer whale tooth, but the tooth had been lost when Bolt fought the Baron, the diabolical despot who had bitten Bolt and left him like this, part penguin and part human. Bolt had survived the battle, and the Baron's remains, if any were left, sat inside the stomach of a sea mammal.

After the fight, Bolt had led the penguins here, hundreds of miles away, far from other people, where they could live in peace. Bolt needed to protect them. It was what he was chosen to do.

Many new penguins had joined the colony since then. Word of the young werepenguin, who treated penguins not as his servants but as his family, had spread far and wide, told from the glubs of fish, the chirps of birds, and the legs of ice crickets.

Bolt stood up, stretched his legs, and strode down the hill. His walk was part waddle and part human, just like the rest of him.

"Good afternoon," barked a nearby penguin, and Bolt smiled. Bolt had never been able to perfect any sort of clear penguin bark, at least not in his human form, but he thought the words *Good afternoon to you* and the penguin smiled, as best a penguin can, which is not much of a smile at all.

Penguins show their emotions through their eyes, mostly. Beaks are not very expressive.

Bolt added, *Have a great day, Lara. I mean Sara. Clara? No, Dara. Sorry about that.*

Most penguins look the same, even to each other, but each have their own unique smell. Bolt's mostly human nose was a weak sniffer compared to a penguin's, so he re-lied on his mind-reading to identify most penguins.

As Bolt walked through the colony, nodding and smil-ing to his brothers and sisters, sometimes messing up their names but not usually, he heard a shout, not a bark but an actual humanlike cry. It took him a few seconds to realize he wasn't imagining it. Yes, it was a human voice, a girl's voice, calling out in the distance.

No, that was impossible. The colony was at least fifty miles from any human town.

"Bolt!"

Or maybe it was possible.

Bolt turned and there, in the horizon, was a girl, wav-ing. A short penguin stood next to her, panting, a small rubber bone in its beak.

Bolt ran toward the figures, his fowl-blood-powered legs skimming across the ice with more traction than if he wore snow boots. He bounded across the snow as the girl with the waving hand, a girl who was about Bolt's age with blonde hair held up by bobby pins, collapsed. She fell first to her knees, and then the rest of her buckled and flopped to the ground like a dead fish. The small penguin next to her bent down beside her and gave a doglike bark.

Bolt squatted on the ice next to the fallen girl, his warm, cold-impervious hands holding her nearly frozen fingers.

"Bolt, I found you," said Annika, her voice a whisper, a small but desperate smile on her ashen face as she closed her eyes and lost consciousness.

TO BE CONTINUED . . .

Acknowledgments

This book went through a long, winding, and curious path. As a result, the number of people who should be acknowledged is lengthy, and many of them are likely to be forgotten here. So if I've forgotten you, please don't take it personally. My memory isn't what it used to licorice sticks. Wait. Was I writing about licorice sticks? I seem to have forgotten.

Oh, right. Acknowledgments. I should have peeked at the heading of this section. First, I need to thank Kendra Levin. Kendra brought this book to life with a passion and eagerness that rivaled my own. Her vision helped shape its current form, a much better form than I could muster on my own, and for that I will always be grateful.

Hannah Mann and Joanna Volpe each played important yet separate roles in this book being what it is today. Thank you for your tireless efforts and assistance, support, and guidance.

This labor of love, heavy on the labor, took the efforts of many talented people. Thank you to illustrator Scott Brown, whose remarkable illustrations far exceeded my expectations; Laura Stiers and Janet Pascal, whose tandem copyediting played a bigger role than I'll ever admit in public; plus designer Kate Renner, Maggie Rosenthal, and the entire team at Viking.

Many people have commented, read, and helped me during the numerous incarnations of this book, and in many different ways. Some of them have given their time and energy to multiple revisions, others have touched only one, and I have kept poor notes on who gave what advice, and when, but each of these people have played valuable roles during the writing of this book: Kym Brunner, Katie Sparks, Veronica Rundell, Cherie Colyer, and Suzanne Slade. They are not in any particular order, just the order I typed them in.

When a book takes a long time to complete, and I know I sound like a broken record harping on the long time it took to finish this, to finish this, to finish this (that's a record skipping joke, which I know is a bit dated), it takes a great deal of patience and understanding from loved ones, so thank you to Lauren, Madelyn, and Emmy. As always, you each have my love and gratitude, which I don't express often enough.

All writers borrow or steal from lots of sources. Hopefully we hide those borrowings well. But still, I'd like to thank some artists whom I have never met, nor likely ever will (as some are deceased and others are beyond my reach), but whose works inspired me while writing this book. I'll use initials to create an air of mystery about these people, because it's always fun to add airs of mystery when you can, which is why I sometimes go grocery shopping in disguise: B.S., A.D., R.D, W.G., R.R., C.D., and M.B. Also F.D. and W.S., sort of.